Bits of Sugar

AND OTHER STORIES

BITS OF SUGAR
AND OTHER STORIES

FINALISTS FROM THE THIRD ANNUAL
GRATEFUL STEPS SHORT STORY CONTEST

GREY WOLFE LAJOIE

SPENCER E. STEVENS

J.S. SOLLAZZO

ROBIN RUSSELL GAISER

EVAN WILLIAMS

BERNIE BROWN

HEATH TOWSON

DENISE OSTLER

JAN FISHER

GRATEFUL STEPS
ASHEVILLE, NORTH CAROLINA

Grateful Steps Foundation
30 Ben Lippen School Road #107
Asheville, North Carolina 28806

Copyright © 2016
Library of Congress Control Number 2019900475
Cover design gy Leslie Stevens
Cover photograph by Paul Looyen

ISBN 978-0-9962490-4-1 Paperback

Printed in the United States of America
at Lightning Source

FIRST EDITION

www.gratefulsteps.org

Contents

Editor's Note

The stories contained in this book were submitted as entries to the third annual short story contest held by Grateful Steps, a traditional, nonprofit, independent pulisher located in Asheville, North Carolina. They were chosen as finalist entries by our staff. Laura Hope-Gill, Assistant Professor of Writing for Lenoir Rhyne University and Director of The Thomas Wolfe Center for Narrative, judged the finalists. She holds an MFA in Poetry from Warren Wilson College MFA Program for Writers and is an NC Arts Fellow for Creative Nonfiction. She selected Grey Wolfe LaJoie's "Bits of Sugar" as the winning entry and Spencer E. Stevens' "Enough to Show" as the runner-up.

Grateful Steps is proud to present these stories in this volume. We know you will enjoy reading them.

Grey Wolfe LaJoie

BITS OF SUGAR

Things had been rough for Daw since the deportation. What worried her most though, her begonia was wilting. For this, more than anything else, she blamed the coward, Bush, and his crusade against the immigrants. Sitting by the window, she whispered Spanish sweetness to the plant, stroked its little red stem, tried even to kiss the small pink petals, so lightly that they wouldn't drop. But it was clear, her flowers were going to die. She let her long loose curls comb through the plant. Daw thought about her papá, the way he would smooth her hair over, speak to her like an adult. Oh, you're only just a jot. I promise, my *pollito*, one day you will be big enough. Why couldn't she stop dreaming about him? She hummed to the begonia, imagined she was like her father for a moment. But she struggled to look at the little potted plant with eyes like his. Really, Daw had never been able to think with her belly the way her father told her to. She stroked the terracotta with the back of her hand anyway, felt the cold clay on her skin, pretended the leafy flits were jiggles of dance. Daw heard her mother coming down the hallway, then the door uncorked and the air ruptured with her mom's voice, spilling in. Cellphone in hand, she spoke hysterically, laughed wildly, going back and forth between English and Spanish. The crazy old gypsy must have been gossiping about another friend, Daw could tell this much. She'd gotten good at muting her mom's chatter, but the talent had gotten rusty while she was away so long, and a few words managed to get in,

"She what? Oh my gaad, Marie, no she did not!"

She rushed over to the window, one arm weighed down by purse and bent by phone, wrapped the free arm around Daw without interrupting her sentence, and then floated into the other room. The hug was like a brief, woolen storm, the coat scratched, the silver pendant popped into Daw's glasses, and the smell drifting over, familiar to her, like butter and honey. Her mother was wearing a lot of purple, and a knocking necklace with thick yellow opals hung from her neck. The same one, Daw noticed, that she had once told her mother was gaudy and tried to hide from her.

"This is just in season." Her mother's words were always hurried, "You just don't keep up, sweetie."

Daw pulled her hair back, pinned it tight. She took the scarlet flower from the sill and carried it into the quiet of the hallway. She sat outside the apartment door on the crummy carpet, dim and uneven, with bald spots, and watched Ecuadorian strangers in heavy coats crinkling quickly by. Her slacks were tight against her thighs in this position, and she felt large in the narrow corridor. It was clear the hallway hadn't been renovated since the early 70s. Burnt orange and lime greens and dusty rubber ferns lined along the dull familiar way. Daw let her plant down easily in the corner, and then laid her head beside it. She let the old carpet rake into her skin, listened to the rain outside. The smell of the filthy carpet twitched and weaved in her mind, worked to pull her into another situation, one where she bounced with her father, tall and thin, by her side. It was rare that memories of him would come back. In this one, the two stand by a lake in the sunshine and feed cheap bread to ducks. She flinches, yanks her hand away, each time a duck tries to reach for the food. She looks up at him shyly, messy hair in the breeze. If you don't want to give it away, don't give it away, *pollito*, she thinks he says, but after that his lips are only moving and the light and the wind of her memory have softened away the details.

***

Those dated, ruined halls had all seemed lavish when initially entering the stark apartment. The first day Daw came back home, almost everything in the apartment was the same as her memory; the spent light fixtures that flickered when she bumped them, the locked, keyless closet doors along one wall, the decorative kerosene lantern on the dinner table, the rumbling refrigerator, the clogged toilet with the splintering wooden seat, the smell of mold. The only thing she had remembered incorrectly was the color of the walls. In her mind, they had always been white. Just white. But she was startled, floored, when she arrived at this apartment and found it swollen with red. There was this strange new way the light from the hazy windows made the cracked wall's surface flush with the glow. On this first day back, the sun rubbed against her all afternoon, pulling morning through to evening. She carried the color around town with her like fuel. But every day since, it rained.

***

After coming back to Guayaquil, Daw had eventually gone back to work at the local chocolate factory, an oxidized shamble of gears and weeds. This factory had been a tuberculosis asylum around the turn of the century, was bought out by Nestlé during the Great Depression, had been slowly collapsing since. The ceiling had caved in decades ago, and the factory had only gone on operating like this, scraping through rain and rust. Each section was made up of thick, black walls that swallowed light and air. Vines had worked their way through diaphragms, around levers, between pistons. Weeds and shrubs worked to deregulate escapements, halt shutters, restrict tone arms. The roots ran along the ground next to various compression hoses, and Daw had to brush away chocolate tar to distinguish between the two. When the coupling coil hissed, steam pushed through the leaves and they fluttered with anger. It was only when a thick enough root had pushed its way through the gears in a machine that the management would rush in with suits, wielding machetes and hack it away from the sunlight. Daw was certain she would contract tetanus within the month and die in a third-world clinic.

Her coworkers all looked at her differently now that she'd been away so long. Her clothing, her accent, even the way she walked, all seemed different. Only one of them hadn't seemed to mind her turtlenecks and pronunciations, Feo, who she worked with in the casting section every Tuesday and Thursday, an energetic little fat man, who liked to talk about sex. The line had been held up in the conching building, and she was trying to use the time to read the newspaper. Feo was texting again. "Ooh hehe!" Daw usually ignored him, she knew if she looked up then he would want to tell her about the latest woman he'd found on the Internet. Feo giggled and bounced with excitement. Officially, Feo was her boss, but he had never given her an order. She wasn't sure why he was so nice to her. He'd told her she seemed "really real."

Feo looked back and forth from his buzzing phone to her.

"Daw! Have you ever fantasized about making love to a pregnant woman?"

The hydraulic equipment picked back up in front of them. He had to yell the last few words over the whirrs and chugs.

It was late. She decided to give in for once. "I guess I've thought about it," she said without looking up.

Feo jiggled a little and said, "I just found this woman who is seven months pregnant and she is desperate. Another one to cross off my list."

Daw put down her paper. "Just, how does that work exactly?" she asked.

Feo furrowed his dependable unibrow. "Sex during pregnancy? I don't know. I guess I just kinda get up in from behind and—"

"No." She stopped him, "No. No, I mean meeting a stranger and then sleeping with her. Do you go out to dinner first? Is it all quick and anonymous?"

One of the propeller pumps began to whine and scrape in the drum. A little red bulb blinked in front of them.

"I mean, I guess it depends on the person. I'm kind of new at the whole thing, but last week I had this wealthy . . . like bondage couple, pretty old folks. Anyway, after we were done and they unzipped me, we had a few drinks and I got to ask questions while I patted their dog." Feo paused and looked down at his hands.

"I am learning so much," he said to himself.

The moaning of machinery deepened and the air pressure gauge in front of them jumped frantically.

"So with the pregnant woman, she's not looking for a father or anything like that?"

Feo set his phone down abruptly, "Jesus, oh god jesus no! I don't want anything to do with kids. So what? You think she's like, trying to manipulate me or something? Oh god, maybe this lifestyle's a bad idea. I don't ever want to be a dad."

She smirked. "What's wrong with parenthood? Don't think you're fit for it?"

Small beads of water began to crawl down the corroded gray metal around them.

"No one's fit to be a parent, Daw." She watched him, waited for the joke to show, but his eyes just stared at her, massive and brown and serious.

"No one's fit to be a parent," he repeated to himself, eyes dry and bulging.

The wads of chocolate started to hum in again, the room depressurized, and with this, Feo went back to his phone, Daw to her newspaper. After that though, she had trouble thinking about the newspaper headlines, about "Operation Iraqi Freedom." Instead, she could only stare into the eyes of George Bush, examine his arched eyebrows, notice the similarities between him and Feo.

***

Each day Daw walked home in the rain, covered in sugary soot and cocoa residue, the sounds of the dark machines still thumping in her head. When she came home, thin and worn after work, her mother was on the phone, shouting at the little television set.

"I'm sure, Marie. Oh, he's a *maricón*. Definitely. Turn on the TV and look! See there. Swine!"

She had a drink in one hand, a fork in the other, the phone tucked into her shoulder. She turned her chin up and spit on the floor near the television. A small string of saliva was left behind on her lips, and it glowed bright white from the television. Daw examined her mother's glass.

"Look at the way he smirks at those sailors."

She cackled and swung her drink around, spilled drips onto her lap.

"Daw, come visit your favorite person!" She thrust her fork toward the TV, rice sprinkling to the floor. Daw walked past her, quickly through the dabs of rice, toward her stranded little flowers. The poor things, leaves had begun to crisp and drop, and the stems had turned dark and scabbing. Only the petals still had any color.

"Have these been watered again?"

Her mother, red lips sipped away, turned in her seat to examine Daw. "Honey, are you . . . wearing running-shoes and dress pants? Oh. Sometimes I just wonder. That's all, sometimes I just wonder," and she turned back again to face the television. On the bulbed TV screen, the American president stood muted on an aircraft carrier, wearing a flight suit, a Mission Accomplished banner behind him. Daw decided it was time to do laundry.

***

Nearly midnight, uneasy in the laundry room of the apartment building, she sat trying to stay awake, and scowling each time the huge orange washer rattled or the sloppy dryer knocked. Every so often she would glance nervously up at a sign:

DO NOT LOAD THE MACHINES AFTER 9 P.M. THANK YOU.

But someone had abandoned one of the machines still full of clothes, leaving her with just one, and she'd needed to put in so many quarters just to get things dry, she told herself it really wasn't her fault at all. The ragged magazine she'd found was full of ads for makeup and it was hard to read, hard just to stay awake, with nothing but the sick strokes of yellow light scratched across the floor. She stirred the mess in her pockets, looking for some distraction. Her phone, with a little blinking icon, a missed call. Someone had called? Why? A voicemail. It was her mother's voice; "Daw? . . . Daw . . . Daw?"—A long antique silence then, from her mother, still speaking to an obsolete answering machine, waiting for her to pick up, and finally, "Call me back Daw." She deleted the message and returned to the empty room's rumbles. After a few more cycles, Daw began to find a rhythm in the knocking, a comfort in the smell of softener. The air in the little room got cool and blue, the big clumsy machines finally found a low hum, and she was washed into a dream.

She was just a little boy, sitting in the sand, trying to learn English by reading Hemingway. It was hard. The sand makes everything hazy. She tried to whisper "Here I am in your life, here you are in mine." But it wouldn't come out. In the distance American soldiers had guns painted to look like toys, and they were moving through the Green Zone, going from home to home, eating all the food, grapes and cheese slipping out of their hands. Following behind one of the soldiers, his daughter, in a little plum dress. Daw was in love with her. That's why Daw was learning English, so that she could be loved by the chubby little American girl and her father. It was hard to watch the soldiers move through, eating all the food. She wanted so badly to join the fat little family and eat with them. She wanted so badly to climb into the plump girl's bed, show her what a little brown boy could do, stiffen her over her thick mattress, baste her.

***

Daw woke up starving. A slender man was slamming dryer doors. For a moment, she thought it was her father. Through the washer steam and sleepy eyes, she could hardly make out the figure gliding across the floor. He was grainy and colorless, like a Dracula from an old silent film. She still had her eyes just pinched open, pretending to sleep as she watched the figure knot his socks with his wiry fingers. He was humming through his twisted nose while he folded. She watched him stop, reach his claws deep into a pocket, pull out a KIT KAT. He balled the candy wrapper up, left it to unscrunch on the folding table. Was she still dreaming? He had a sweet smile. He started to mutter things to himself. At first, they were whispers to himself, things like, "Where did I put that paisley shirt?" or "Oh, I hope I didn't shrink this." But soon she realized that he was speaking to her; "Don't want you to catch a cold in here." His voice was high and sweet and Southern, like a peach. Every one of his words was a bite. He bent down and turned a knob on the radiator. Dracula hovered toward her, raised his arms and draped a leather jacket slowly over her before disappearing with his basket. Daw waited until she couldn't hear his light steps any longer, and then she rose quickly to examine the chocolate wrapper. She scowled. It must have been getting so late, the sky seemed to shift from black to dim blue. She decided to leave a note, composed with a strict and forceful hand. She hung it above a washer and stepped back to admire it:

REMINDER: ALL TENANTS SHOULD NOT BE USING THE MACHINES AFTER HOURS. ALSO: WE'VE NOTED A RECENT LITTERING PROBLEM. PLEASE REFER TO OUR POLICY ON THIS.

Finally, she smoothed out the KIT KAT wrapper and taped it to the note.

Holding her breath, Daw snuck slowly back into the apartment. In the living room, her mother slept, the light of the television still showering her. Daw slinked into the kitchen. Opened the fridge, nothing. The freezer, only TV dinners. She nudged through to the backs of the shelves, but there was nothing of nutritional value. The cabinets? Nearly empty, but at least there was one can of soup. Fine, but when she lifted it, the thing was nearly weightless. She pulled it from the back. In the pale light, it gleamed gold. In quivering, bony scribbles it said *pedacitos de azucar*. Bits of sugar. She glanced over to her mother, looked back to the can, and slipped quickly out into the hallway. Daw made sure no one was coming down the hallway before she opened the soup can's lid with her teeth. For a moment, she thought it was some slab of stone or canvas, but inside were little slips of paper, rolled up together so long that they had yellowed and stiffened up into each other, creating one thick block of paper. She had to split them away from each other, like layers of bark. The first thing she read was a thin poem, her mother's handwriting;

10/6/71 - for P
maybe to make music
out of my burst eardrum.
there is also, potentially
the gash across my arm.
your car key slid through
leaving wet pink flesh exposed
and i watched the red glide in after

as if afraid of light.
a sweet shadow on my skin
i might look at until death
and revive a smile.

it seems our ghostly touch
has overdosed on gravity.
so heavy,
like a t-shirt worn swimming.
perhaps someone could
turn the knob on the lantern
of kerosene, until the shadows
have left from under your eyes.
and if we're lucky,
the glass chimney will blacken
and explode.
and everyone at the dinner table
will be covered pink, in sweet little scars.

Daw pulled out another one;

4/25/73
dear P, last night i dreamed you were leaving,
you were slipping into a glass hole in the ground
and all of my things were attached to your skin.
you had on that jacket and those glasses you used
to wear. you were telling me that you had to go
and that you wouldn't be back and i knew you
had to but i didn't want you to go.

There were so many. She decided to read one more;

7/2/75
P, i worked so hard to be open for you, but you
always kept things at arm's length. i could never
forget you. you act like i'm over you and i could
move on if you'd just let me, but that isn't how it is.
if you want to leave the country again and find
some new life, fine. you say you can't forget me
and you love me and you're still attracted to me

and all the bullshit. it seems like you have already forgotten me though. so go ahead and leave me pregnant and alone. i want to ignore you, to let you experience life without me and feel alone and remember that i'm who you should be with. but i don't know the trick as well as you. i have had moments where i yearn to hurt you back. but that's not what i want. i want my life back.

Daw pulled the rest of the papers out of the can, pushed them all back together and stuffed the brick of writing into her shirt, a secret lump, pressed against her chest. She tiptoed into the apartment again, came up to her sleeping mother. It was too cold. Her mother's breath looked like fumes of exhaust, she shivered out such quick, heavy breaths. The drink was crooked in her hand, dripping the last sip into the floor. The TV still glowed against her skin, and its gray light made her seem so pale, the color of aspirin. She was smiling in her sleep. A sad smile, Daw thought.

***

At the factory the next day, between the gnashing of metal teeth and through the screams of pipeline tracheas, Daw thought about her father. She tried to remember his face, but could only recall his hands. What was it that he used to say all the time? *Whether you like it or not, alone is something you'll be quite a lot!* That couldn't be right. No. After lunch, Feo was trying to tell her all about the pregnant woman. About the weight of the stomach, how he had felt a kick during sex, the way the globe stared at him like a third eye. He tried to explain, with wide eyes, how fatherhood had crossed the woman's mind. How she'd wanted him to help with her prenatal yoga. But Daw couldn't focus. She could only think about the letters, about her father, about Dracula. It was Feo's scream she noticed first,

"Daw, watch it!"

She looked, and a pool of blackened, flaming chocolate muck had strayed from the line, toward her, had begun absorbing her hand, smoking and popping and hissing into skin. Her first thought was of ducks.

On the phone, her mother's friend Marie answered first, did most of the talking. Told Daw that her mom was in the bathroom, would be right out. Told her about the time Marie's older brother was burned when they were just teenagers. How her brother and his friend were playing with methylated spirits, how methylated spirits have invisible flame, who knew they had an invisible flame? Tipped the can over and had his whole lower side engulfed. Told her about the medical bills and how they prayed for him. Told her she should find a cold compress. "Well, anyway, here's your mom," she said.

"Honey, sweetie, what is it? Why are you calling?"

"Mamá, I burned my hand," Daw said faintly.

"How bad is it?" she said. "What color?" Her mother's voice was quick and accurate.

"The guys went to go get ice. Should they go get ice?"

"How bad is the pain?"

"I feel sick."

"How long ago did this happen?"

"Twenty minutes ago, maybe . . . maybe an hour. I - I'm not sure."

"Daw, what color is it?"

"It's wet. It's so shiny. What color is the burn? There's white. A lot of white. There's a lot in the middle. Is that my bone?"

"That isn't your bone. Bone isn't white while it's still inside you."

"It hurts so much—"

"That's okay, that means the burn hasn't reached your nerve endings. What is the color around the white? Is it black?"

"Should I find an ointment?"

"Not yet. Is it black around the burn, honey?"

"No, it's really red like a, a blister, like a—Oh."

There was a long silence, and then her mother repeated, "Daw. Daw. Daw.—Hey!"

"Oh, I closed my eyes for a second. It hurts so bad."

"You're in shock. Have the others come back yet?"

"I burned my hand." Daw said gently. Sadly.

"Are you still alone?"

"I think I should go look for a cold compress."

"You need to go to the hospital. Are you by yourself?" Her mother's voice was soft.

"Should I call an ambulance?"

"Ambulances are too expensive. Someone should drive you. Where are the others?"

"I . . . I think . . . I don't remember," Daw said pitifully.

"If it's not black and it's not numb, everything should be fine as long as you get to the hospital . . ." Her mother's speech started to slow; she seemed to talk more to herself. "But then—There isn't anyone there with you?—Stay there. I'm coming over."

SPENCER E. STEVENS

ENOUGH TO SHOW

IT WAS NOT YET DECEMBER AND MARCUS ALREADY DESPISED THE cold that found its way into his bones moments after he had stepped out the door. He stood at the corner of Sherman and Fitch Street with his hands shoved into his pockets, his hoodie pulled down to his eyebrows, covering the short Afro he had inherited from the father he barely remembered. The only visible part of the boy was his green eyes, which glowered at his fellow high schoolers as they waited for the morning bus. When he left Tucson, Marcus felt the sun beating sweat down his brow. But now he stood in the fifty-six-degree wind of a Northern California morning, where the morning dew clung to his skin and clothes, sucking away his last bit of heat.

A distinct yet unfamiliar feeling tugged at the back of his mind—the same feeling he would feel on vacation in a place that was of high contrast to home. Incomprehensibly, just one month ago, his family had lived a different life in Arizona. A fact that Marcus struggled with now. He had gone to a public high school that had over two thousand people. He now attended a private school with less than seven hundred students.

Even more unimaginable, was that he had to live this strange life without his mother, who had died one month ago.

Marcus spent the majority of his days in the back of classrooms, head on his arm, sleeping through lectures given by people from this other planet. School, to Marcus, consisted of bumbling back and forth along the one story building in which this small community educated their youth, aside from occasionally being called on by his teachers to answer a question that had been covered while he was sleeping.

Marcus was staring at the clock above his calculus teacher. It was his last period of the day and the clock seemed to be decelerating in speed. He chuckled sarcastically to himself about the reference to the calculus lesson he had just made. *Question,* thought Marcus. *If every minute gains five seconds, will I ever get out of here?*

As he stared at the clock, he slowly became cross-eyed and he let his vision remain blurry for a while before he blinked. The fluorescent lights were reflecting off of the white walls and pulsing toward him even when he closed his eyes. Marcus could almost taste how many times the same dry air had been recycled through the heat ducts. His head was propped on his hand, his elbow on the table. He fought the urge to yawn, wondering vaguely if his fatigue was caused by grief.

When Marcus opened his eyes he was in the passenger seat of a car. It was the same car that had dropped him off and picked him up from school for years. The city streets were passing by in a blur. Looking sideways he saw his mother, her neat business attire and pulled back hair, an orderly contrast to their car. Its stained and torn upholstery and scratched body had driven the price down and made it affordable for them.

Marcus's heart started to beat faster, and he wasn't quite sure why. "Hey, Mom?" He asked loudly, but she didn't respond. "Mom!"

"What?" She turned toward him, taking her eyes off the road and pulling her attention away from the light that had just turned red. The truck driver didn't see their car in time to blow his horn. But Marcus saw the truck and the driver hurtling closer and closer to his mother whose attention was still on him. And then she was gone.

"No!" Marcus's head hit the window on his right and his eyes shot open. The girl sitting next to him had her hand covering her mouth. The white lights of the classroom were outlining her red hair in a faint glow. Marcus's head lay on the table. His chin must have fallen from his hand while he was dreaming and smacked down into the cold smooth desk. He quickly sat up. Every single person in the class was staring at him.

"What was that, Marcus?" His teacher had turned from the board to give him a glare for disrupting his class. Panicked, Marcus realized that he had yelled out loud. He stared at the teacher. Then quickly picking up his books bag he ran, out of the classroom, down the hall, and out the door where the cold air was, for once, as welcome as an old friend.

When he finally arrived home, he was greeted at the door by his grandmother's scarlet face. Marcus tried to swallow.

"Do you want to tell me where you were today? I got a call from your teacher saying you left class and didn't come back." His grandmother's mouth was puckered in disapproval, giving even more wrinkles to her pale face. Her hair resembled white cotton candy and her eyes were too watery as they gazed up at him with barely disguised disappointment.

Marcus wasn't even going to try to make up an excuse for what had happened. Everything he would say would sound crazy. "I just had to go for a walk." All of his adrenaline gone, he now felt drained and even more tired than before.

His grandmother berated him with questions such as, "What do you think you're doing with your life?" and "Do you think you're more special than the others?" for which Marcus had no answers, so he made a move toward his room. "Don't you move until you've answered me!" Grandmother shouted.

"It was just too much! Anyway school is pointless. We're all going to die in the end anyway," said Marcus, his dark green eyes meeting his grandmother's light blue.

"School is not pointless unless you want to have a miserable life. Do you want to have a miserable life?" queried Grandmother.

"I don't know. It doesn't matter." He could no longer look her in the eyes.

"It doesn't matter? Marcus, I know you're grieving, I am too, but your mother wouldn't have wanted you to throw your life away. Your grandfather and I are your parents now and we are not going to let you do this to yourself."

Marcus focused on his breathing. One. Two. Three. Four. His fingernails digging into his palm took attention away from his eyes that were begging him to cry. No. Five. Six.

"Okay. Go." His grandmother's face softened in resignation as she reached out and gingerly patted his shoulder.

Seven. Eight.

"You'll be late for your lesson." She cleared her throat.

Marcus turned toward the door, then paused, "You said you were grieving too, but it doesn't seem like it. I mean, I barely see Grandpa."

"Marcus, your grandfather doesn't want you to see him upset. Every time he looks at you he sees your mother's eyes."

Eight. Eight. Eight. What comes next? Marcus gritted his teeth. He sighed and turned around to step out into the grey afternoon. He didn't care if he was late to his piano lesson. He hadn't had a clean attendance record there either. With the same bag he brought to school slung over his shoulder, Marcus walked as slowly as possible down the nearly empty streets. The locals were smart to stay inside during such weather, he thought. Dark clouds had been moving in to blanket the sky since the morning and it looked like a storm was brewing.

Halfway through town, Marcus stopped to watch the bus he was supposed to be on roll past, feeling relieved. The gratitude of not being on the bus had just crept up when thunder cracked down from the clouds, which were seeming more ominous than before. Marcus looked around him for a warm place to relieve his extremities of their numbness.

The coffee shop Marcus found was in a small, one-story building that was wedged between two larger buildings. A large portion of its floor space was crowded with odds and ends for sale. Marcus ordered a coffee and meandered around the pile-like displays. An old typewriter, some figurines and a rack of hats were in a pile beside wooden toys some dolls and books that looked to be from the 50s. In the back were racks of vintage clothes that might have belonged to his grandparents years ago.

The basement of the coffee shop was much the same. One corner was crowded with furniture, antique mixed with modern. Marcus walked over to a small side table that caught his eye. Its top was a half circle, the outer edge painted to look like piano keys. In between it's wrought iron legs, a series of music notes welded along lines represented sheet music with a wiry treble clef in the center. Wow Marcus thought, running his hands along its edges. Mom would have loved this table. She played piano like it was the only thing she lived for. His grandparents thought he inherited her musical skills. They thought wrong. This train of thought reminded Marcus of the exact place he was not at this moment. Piano lessons.

He had first met Albert, his piano instructor, three weeks ago during the first and last piano lesson he had been to.

The receptionist for the music school had been typing intently when Marcus arrived. She quickly turned her attention to him. Her chestnut hair was in a tight bun, the same way his mother had worn hers. Her red-stained lips stretched into a smile that made her face expand, revealing teeth that were the same white as her blouse. She directed him to the only piano teacher in the building, which was on the top floor.

As Marcus ascended the steps with as little grace and as much noise as he could, he passed endless doors with various genres of music being played by more instruments than Marcus thought existed.

"Pricks," he muttered. "They must not have a life."

By the time Marcus reached the door marked 32D, he was panting, his previous sulkiness forgotten in his attempt to stretch out the cramp in his right side.

As Marcus opened the door a strong smell hit him that could only be described as old paper. Marcus's eyes adjusted quickly to the rooms dim lighting and he could see the source of the musty odor. Directly across the room were floor to ceiling book shelves, their papery occupants looked to have originated from the 1700s, and Marcus was surprised that they were still intact. They were all different shades of brown and grey and in various stages of decay. To his left was a grand piano, and behind that was a wall that was almost entirely filled with windows, though barely any light escaped through the thick moth-eaten drapes. To his right was a very large wooden desk, the legs of which ended in clawed feet on the floor, harboring a man who had thick black hair that was long overdue for a trim. The man was bending over a book, studying it so closely that his nose nearly touched the pages.

Marcus closed the door and stood in the center of the room panting. "You've got to do something about the stairs."

"Ah. It gets the blood flowing to the mind and fingers, preparing you to play with magnificence!" the man cried out without moving from his position hovering over the book. "That was only four flights." The man sighed. "Marcus, I presume." Only then did the he look up, eyeing Marcus with the same intensity that he had given the book. The man's hair fell to his shoulders and his inquisitive eyes looked younger than the lines etched in his face, though he was probably not yet forty.

Shocked, Marcus rudely asked, "How old are you?" Confused at the contrast between the room and its owner.

Not put off by the boy's lack of manners, the man smiled. "Thirty-seven."

"Hm." Marcus noticed that next to the desk was a couch, which he sat on without invitation, surprisingly sinking, so that his knees were above his waist.

The instructor continued to eye Marcus over the rim of his coffee mug, and when he put it down, said, "Music can age you and keep you young all at the same time."

Marcus nodded. *That makes sense. How wise!* he thought sarcastically.

"So shall we get started?" Albert stood up and walked to the piano, motioning for Marcus to follow. "I think we should aim for 'Clair de Lune.'"

Over the span of the next hour, Albert attempted to teach Marcus the beginning notes, which proved most difficult. They spent several minutes on one chord, only to have it forgotten as soon as they moved on to the next.

After the allotted time of an hour and a half, Albert said, "Well that seems to be all the time we have today." He stood and ran his hand over his hair, moving back toward his desk. "Will I see you next week?"

"Sure," Marcus replied curtly. That was the last lesson he had gone to, and after that, Marcus spent the hour and a half every week walking through the town which seemed to have gotten stuck in the past. Marcus assumed Albert had not called his grandparents so he would continue to be paid for lessons. *It was a win-win,* Marcus thought happily.

When enough time had passed, Marcus left the coffee shop to go home. The long walk was a pleasant one, despite the cold, and it gave him a sense of freedom. Before Marcus had closed the door between the cold and himself, he heard his grandmother call to him. "Marcus! Why didn't you tell us?"

"Tell you what?" Marcus felt a lump begin to grow in his throat. Albert had probably called his grandmother to report the missed lessons.

She came around the corner to where Marcus was removing his damp boots and waved an opened envelope. "About your Christmas recital! You were going to tell us weren't you? Oh we are so looking forward to it!"

"Oh. Right. It must have slipped my mind." Marcus had not heard of the performance. He supposed Albert would have told him in one of the lessons he did not attend. "What day is it? I forgot." He swallowed.

"Christmas Eve, silly. That's such an easy day to remember." She scoffed, teasingly. "It will be such a great Christmas present to hear you play the piano. What piece have you chosen?"

"Uh, well . . . it's a surprise, Grandma, so I really can't tell you anything."

"Well, we're very excited. Grandpa and I wouldn't miss it for the world." His grandmother pulled him in for a hug.

Marcus, still shivering from the cold, began to sweat. "Yeah. Hey, speaking of practice, I forgot my sheet music. I need to go back and get it."

"Oh, of course," she said letting go of him. "Do you need me to drive you there? There's no buses running for a while."

"No. I'll go tomorrow after breakfast."

***

The following morning was a Saturday, and at 8:00, Marcus was stepping once more into the wind. "God. I'm getting tired of this cold." He watched his words drift away from him in small clouds.

Marcus knocked repeatedly on door 32D until a frustrated "One moment!" came through the door. It was opened by a tired looking Albert holding a mug of black coffee.

"How can you drink that stuff?" Marcus gagged.

"Well, good morning to you too. How may I uh . . . help you?" Albert yawned and scratched his chin, which was shadowed by neglect of a razor.

"You could let me in, you know." When Albert didn't respond Marcus continued, "I need a piece for the show." Albert, still blinking away last night, didn't move. "I need you to teach me something for the Christmas show. I don't care what as long as it sounds good. I'll do whatever you say, just please help me."

Albert furrowed his brow and considered the frantic boy for a moment. "Very well. Okay . . . let's start with something new. It will be slow and simple, but I think we could make it work."

Albert let him inside. Marcus decided not to say anything about the blanket that was strewn on the ratty couch alongside a pillow that had an indent from a sleeping head.

"Do you think we'll have enough time?" Marcus was already seated at the piano.

"If you try, Marcus, then yes, we will."

They sat side by side, Albert playing the notes first and Marcus repeating them. Eventually Marcus could play the entire piece slowly and with mistakes but completely through nonetheless, reading off the sheet music. Nearly two hours had gone by unnoticed before Albert's first student of the day knocked on the door, surprising them both.

"Practice tonight. Come back tomorrow morning same time and we will resume." Albert collected the sheets of music, handed them to Marcus and directed his next student toward the piano.

***

Marcus didn't know a whole lot about his father, only what his mother could tell him, and she told him all that she could remember. They met at Juilliard and he played the cello. She had a lot of pictures of him, since they were both hobby photographers. Most of the pictures they had developed in black and white. Marcus had albums of them. Close ups of his mother's hands on a piano, or his father's head resting on the neck of his cello, his springy hair a chaos around the calm of his concentrating face. Marcus had always been curious about who his father was, and he had been thinking about this strange man more and more since his mother's death. His grandparents had tried to find him to tell him about Marcus's mother's death. But just like their daughter, they failed to find him, and at the funeral, Marcus could feel an empty space next to him on the pew where he knew that his father should be. This man that he was tied so closely to was somewhere out in the world, not knowing that he was his son's last hope of having a parent.

***

The next day, Marcus was back in the piano room, sitting at the bench and racking his brain to remember what he had learned yesterday.

Exasperated, Albert cried out, "You didn't practice did you? I told you that if you didn't practice you would forget all that you learned!" Albert pressed one of his palms firmly on his forehead and grabbed his hair with his fingers. "Try again."

"It's okay. I'm just really tired. It will take me a second to warm up," a determined Marcus replied.

"Tired? You're not playing well because you're too tired? I can't believe this." Albert slammed the book with the sheet music closed. "Look, you were the one who wanted this, but I cannot waste my time on someone who won't give a little bit of his time in return. You can come back once you've gained some initiative, and not until then."

Marcus stood up and stomped toward the door, slamming it closed behind him as hard as he could, hoping some of Albert's old books would fall off the shelf.

***

A light knocking came from Marcus's bedroom door. "Can I come in?"

"Sure."

His grandmother was carrying a cardboard box whose corners were stained and whose lips were turned down like the ears of a disappointed dog. She sat down on the bed and handed Marcus a small package that was sitting on top of the box. The brown paper was neatly wrapped in a rectangle. It was addressed to Marcus with the address of the grandparent's house. There was no name to say who it was from, just a return address to a P.O. box somewhere in Washington state.

"We just got this in the mail today. It's addressed to you. Do you know who it could be from?" his grandmother asked.

Marcus eyed the little brown package and shook his head. He took it and sat next to his grandmother and began to unravel the layers of brown paper. As the covering fell away, it revealed a picture in a plain wooden frame. There was a girl and a boy in the picture who seemed to be about Marcus's age. The girl's blond hair was framing her face and her wide smile invited warmth into Marcus's heart. His mother's joy was captured perfectly, and he smiled back at the young version of her. He did not recognize the boy immediately because the boy was wearing sunglasses and leaning toward the edge of the picture. But of course it was Marcus's father

As Marcus went to set down the picture, he felt something on the back of it. A small envelope with his name handwritten on it. It contained a piece of paper that seemed to have been folded and refolded many times. The print on it was small and cramped. It read:

Dear Marcus,

If you're reading this letter, then I was right that you had gone to live with your grandparents. I'm sure your mother has told you a lot about me, but there are some things I know she would have hidden from you, and I think that I should tell you them now. When your mother and I met, we

were very young and I was into some bad stuff. She loved me so she overlooked my drug use, but when I saw you for the first time, right after you were born, I knew I wouldn't be able to be your father. I would just end up hurting both of you. Getting clean wasn't a choice for me back then so I left. My addictions got worse and I was in and out of homeless shelters for ten years. Almost seven years ago your mother sent a letter to my parents to give to me the next time they saw me. The letter was long and detailed about every great thing you had done in the years since I had left. That's when I checked into rehab. I don't remember making the decision, and it wasn't an easy road, but I can happily say I am doing very well. I am writing you now because I heard about your mother's death from my parents just a week ago. I wanted to write you in the hopes that you wouldn't feel so alone and to tell you that I have learned it is not the person's dying that defines their end. It is what you do to remember them that counts.

I wish I could have been there to see you grow up, but I was afraid that all I would do is disappoint you and your mother. I'm not perfect. I don't expect you to understand or forgive me. I just wanted to tell you that I love you as I loved your mother, and I wish you the best, always.

**

Marcus leaned on his hand to cover his mouth as he read the letter again. The first time. This was the first time in almost seventeen years that Marcus or anybody had heard from his father. His eyes became blurry. One. Two. Three. His grandmother put an arm around him and pulled him into a hug. And there they sat in a tight embrace until both of them could not cry any longer. She ran her hand over his hair, then leaned down to pick up the other box that she had brought in.

"These are some home videos." She lifted the flaps of the box to reveal organized rows of DVDs and VHSs. "All of these have your mother in them. Your grandfather had all the VHSs copied onto DVDs a few years ago so you can watch them on the TV in here."

Marcus nodded and stared at the box that had been passed to him. "Thank you."

His grandmother nodded, smiled, then left without another word, closing the door softly behind her.

Marcus started with the earliest movies of his mother as a baby. He watched her first smiles and her first steps, he opened the presents with her at Christmas, and he saw her show off her new dress for the eighth grade dance. It was late into the night now and Marcus could barely keep his eyes open. He was crouching below the TV to remove the current DVD when he heard a tune so familiar that he didn't notice it at first. He leaned back to see, full screen, his mother sitting at a piano, the first notes of "Clair de Lune" still echoing from the TV. Shock woke him out of whatever tiredness he had felt before, and he stared wide eyed at the TV.

She played much better than he could ever hope to. Even though the footage was grainy, he could see her long, pale fingers fluttering over the keys as if the song was something so delicate it might break if it were breathed on.

When the performance was finished and his mother stood up to bow, Marcus no longer felt the need for sleep. He ran over to his keyboard and pulled it onto the bed. He sat in front of it and replayed the video of his mother, he played the first notes trying to match the motions she made. After he finished the first measure, he paused the video, then played the beginning again by himself, then pressed play again and watched for the next notes. This back and forth practice went on for hours until he finally played the last note and collapsed backward on the bed, falling into a deep sleep and, for the first time since his mother's death, Marcus's sleep was void of nightmares.

***

The next morning Marcus took out a piece of lined paper and a pencil and sat down in front of the desk that was at the foot of his bed. He began to write.

Dear Dad,
You are right. I understand your reasons, but I don't think I can forgive you yet. Mom and I both needed you. For good or for bad, nobody could have taken your place. She loved you, and I needed you as a father. I still need you. We tried to find you to tell you that Mom had died, but we couldn't. You missed her funeral, and you should have been there. But you had missed a lot so we didn't expect you to show up after sixteen years. I have a piano recital on Christmas Eve. I am hoping I can at least get by without completely embarrassing myself or falling down on stage. I don't have the musical talent that you or Mom had, so I don't know what I'm doing in lessons anyway. My teacher, like everyone, eventually gave up trying to teach me. I'm sorry for what you've been through, but I wish you would have at least written. I don't know what else I can say.
Marcus

***

Breathe. Breathe. Breathe. Marcus' lungs disagreed with his mind and they tried to race along with his heart. He wiped his palms onto his brand new pants that his grandmother had bought for him for this show. The piano seemed too big, and he hadn't looked at the audience yet, though by the sound of it, the theatre was packed. The director announced Marcus' name and then he sat down on the piano bench. You know this song. He thought It's in your blood. Marcus dared to look up at the audience. He scanned the sea of unfamiliar faces for the ones of his grandparents, who had reserved front row tickets. He looked up and down the front once then twice. They weren't there. The spotlights looked like the headlights of the truck before it crashed into Mom's car. Marcus thought bitterly, *I wonder if she would even want me to do this. It was her song after all.* Marcus stood up to leave and that's when he saw them.

Two figures making their way down the center aisle, the first his grandfather, the second his grandmother. But there was a third person with them. They were too much in the shadow for Marcus to see them clearly, but once they came closer to the stage, the profile was given a face and a name. Marcus was frozen standing up, just about to push back the piano bench. He was staring into the face of his father, and his father was staring back at him, also frozen. His father lifted a hand as if to wave, and then put it back down, deciding against it. He shoved his hands into his pockets, blinking as if he had just woken up. Marcus could hear his heart beating in his ears as his father took a seat next to his grandparents.

Marcus sat back down on the piano bench and adjusted himself. He placed his fingers in the familiar position, and he began to play.

J.S. SOLLAZZO

GOLDEN YEARS

MASON HAD BEEN TOO BUSY LIVING HIS LIFE TO NOTICE THAT most of it had passed him by. The years had rolled away like the view from a runaway train, a kaleidoscope of commutes and work and weekends mowing the grass and vacations that never quite lived up to their expectations.

After he had retired from his job and his kids were gone, he realized that nothing fit anymore. His house was too big, his pants too tight, his skin too loose. He felt pains in his bones that he never felt before and his eyes and ears could no longer be trusted. He was tired until it was time to sleep, then he lay awake for hours, his mind searching for answers to questions he had never before thought to ask. He'd watch his wife sleep in the dim light and try to remember the things that had made him marry her, tried to remember the beautiful woman she had been before the wrinkles and fat, before she smelled of talcum powder, before she let her luscious blond hair turn blue, before she turned out the lights before getting undressed. But it was hopeless. The lust she had once invoked in him, so strong it had made his mouth water and his body quiver, had been gone so long that he had forgotten it ever existed.

They had two children, both grown, both living far away. They do what is required of them, calling on the proper holidays, visiting on

Christmas. He barely knows his grandchildren; they seem like new people each time he sees them, the year separating their visits filled with growth spurts and evolving interests that make him promise to see them more often, a promise he never keeps.

***

One otherwise uneventful day, he decided to go for a walk. Not for his health—Mason was not imaginative enough to believe that exercise or vitamins or anything else could stop the disease of old age from running its inevitable course—but to escape the silence. He and his wife had run out of things to say to each other years before. The low drone of the talk shows on TV and the clanking of dishes from his wife's obsessive cleaning were slowly driving him crazy.

It became a daily habit. He walked in his neighborhood, a tree-lined, geometric grid of middle class homes sitting on well-manicured lawns. He'd wave at his neighbors and stop at the park to watch the children play their seasonal sports. Each time he went out, he walked a little farther, until he was soon making multiple loops around the neighborhood. He lost weight and the muscles in his thighs and calves turned taut and lean.

Sleep was no longer a problem. His eyes grew heavy before the nightly news came on and within minutes of climbing into bed he was dreaming. His dreams were mostly memories, revisits to random moments in his life, this time armed with the knowledge of all that will occur after and he said and did things in those dreams that he wished he had done the first time.

One of his dreams involved a woman he had met many years before on a business trip to the desultory plains of Wichita, Kansas. Her name was Lisa and she had full lips and eager brown eyes and thick dark hair that she obsessively ran through her manicured fingers. She had joined him and several colleagues for drinks at the hotel bar where most of them were staying, and, several hours and martinis later, he found himself alone with her. The lights were low, and the bar was empty, and she touched him and looked at him in a way that let him know he could share her bed. But he couldn't shake away the images of his still-pretty wife and still-young children and he went to bed alone.

But in his dream he followed to her room and did things to her that he thought he had forgotten how to do. When he awoke in a hot sweat and with a pulsing erection he thought he was still dreaming. It was his first erection in more years than he cared to remember and he didn't know what to do with it. So he simply waited, willing his long-missing friend to go away so that he could relieve his full bladder.

That morning he walked farther and faster than ever, until his shirt was drenched and his legs quivered. There was something inside him, something hot and hungry, something frightening and exciting and vaguely familiar that pushed him through the miles.

That evening after dinner he and his wife both settled into their perfect depressions in the couch to watch the night's sitcoms. Mason caught a whiff of his wife's powdery scent. It was a smell he had grown accustomed to, an unsexy smell she had adopted sometime shortly after menopause and its requisite weight gain. But tonight it stirred something in him, made him remember the sweet, soapy scent of her youth. A fire ignited in him, a heat he had not felt since the Reagan years. He put his arms around his wife and kissed her on the neck, inhaling the pheromones hiding under her perfume.

His wife jumped as if electrocuted and let out a sharp squeal. She pushed him away and involuntarily put her hands to her throat, clutching the collar of her housedress. "Mason, what's gotten into you?" There was fear and confusion in her voice.

It made Mason angry. But when he looked into her wide, panicked eyes he realized for the first time that they had not aged in all their years together. They were the same bottomless brown eyes that had first made him notice her when they had both been teenagers. They were as beautiful now as they had been then.

"I love you. I still love you," he said, surprised that it was true.

He could see her mind working behind those eyes, trying to remember their long-ago lives, and he waited until her face softened and she smiled a smile that erased fifty years from her face. "I love you too," she said, and when he leaned in to kiss her, she met him halfway. It was a hungry kiss, the kind of kiss they had once taken for granted.

After a while he took her by the hand and led her into their bedroom and they used it for something other than sleeping for the first time in many wasted years. It had been so long since they had last made love that it was as exciting as the first time. They fell asleep in each other's arms.

She walked with him the next morning, and every morning after that.

Robin Russell Gaiser

I'LL FLY AWAY

Kurt sang like a choir boy. His tall, burly physique and his career as a state trooper didn't match his voice, a sweet, high tenor harmonizing from memory. When he sang, his blue eyes sparkled and his gruffness melted away like ice on a sunny day. He was retired now, and in poor health. I met him at church and encouraged him to join the choir. We were members now for two years at the typical, small, white clapboard, New England-style Presbyterian Church. Its wide open, red double doors welcomed new choir members along with all sorts of combinations of folks.

"I can't read music." Kurt repeatedly apologized for not accepting my invitation to Tuesday choir practice.

"Just show up and try it. I can help you."

Sure enough he walked right up to the choir loft, his cane tapping the wooden steps, ready for rehearsal on the following Tuesday at 4 p.m.

"What do I need?" He was more forthright than I imagined.

My mother, the choir director, scrambled to assemble music into a black folder, and passed him the packet along with a list of music for the month, handwritten on notebook paper in her somewhat illegible script. She was eighty years old at the time. Kurt was seventy-five, but his multiple heart operations had aged him.

Thus began a love affair over music between me and Kurt. When he became discouraged about the difficulty of the choir music, I calmed him down, helped him find his notes. His natural ability to harmonize, singing his own made-up music high above the melody, actually prevailed over the written notes most of the time, but no one cared. My mother told him, "Kurt, just do what you do," a real stretch for her, a college -educated singer and pianist. But she knew his presence and his beautiful voice lent a special ambiance to the front of the church where he sat with the choir each Sunday morning.

Kurt approached me one July morning after church, carrying a bulging manila folder. He opened it to show me his collection of favorite hymns, gospel tunes, folksongs, the copies now dog-eared and yellowing.

"My mother and I sang these together. I stood next to her as she played the piano, and I think that's where I learned to sing harmony. I go back to these copies for the words."

Besides church choir and working toward my CMP, another outlet for my musical energy was forming a music committee within the local arts network. Its reputation had plummeted along with its bank account when the former president resigned under suspicious circumstances. When New York City folks migrated north in the summer to their camps on the lake, I seized this opportunity to begin a concert series featuring affordable professional musicians along with an open mic in the Village Park on Sunday afternoons. I hoped the well-heeled summer people, along with the local folk might bring picnics and lawn chairs and toss in a few bucks when we passed the hat during intermission.

"Would you sing with me at open mic?" Kurt eyed me for a reaction. "I've never sung in public, except in church, but I think I can do it if you sing with me," he said.

"Sure. What do you have in mind?" I said, rather surprised at his request and my quick response.

" 'Precious Memories.' And maybe 'I'll Fly Away.' "

"I love those songs. Great choices. We'll need to rehearse. When are you free?"

Kurt's wife drove him out to my lake house a couple times a week until we felt secure in the music. I played guitar and sang melody. He sang his signature harmony. We practiced the songs over and over, more for his confidence than for his musicality.

Our turn on Sunday afternoon at open mic arrived. We sang late in the program. Kurt was nervous, sweating and out of breath. I worried about the performance placing too much strain on his fragile heart.

Lots of church members plus his family sat in the audience, knowing what a big day this was for Kurt. When our act was announced, my husband jumped up out of his lawn chair in the front row to aid Kurt as he wobbled up the rickety stage stairs using his cane to steady him. I followed, and we stepped into place on the stage before the microphones. He looked at me, his expression asking, "Do you think I can do this?" I nodded with a grin and began the guitar intro. His nerves settled down once he began singing, his liquid tenor voice soaring over top of my melody. *Precious mem'ries, unseen angels, sent from somewhere to my soul; how they linger, ever near me, and the sacred scenes unfold.*

He really wowed the crowd, sang his best. And he easily slid into our next number. *Some bright morning when this life is o'er, I'll fly away. To a home on God's celestial shore, I'll fly away.* The lyrics rattled me a bit. I wondered if they affected him. Did he know he was singing his own farewell with these words? When the applause broke out, I stepped back from the mic and watched him in his glory. He was glowing, center stage, soaking up the attention.

After this success, Kurt's desire to perform at open mic amplified, but his health declined. He never did sing a solo, but through the summer open mics with me by his side, he overcame any shyness he had about singing in public.

By the fall his breath and his energy level from his inoperable heart condition finally robbed him of his singing voice. He was unable to navigate the steps up to the choir loft and with regret, handed in his black choir folder and dropped out of choir. His cardiologist said Kurt's heart could give out any day.

But Kurt had one last request.

"I'd like to sing 'I'll Fly Away' with you and Heidi in church. Maybe three part harmony. She already agreed, if you will."

Heidi was his youngest daughter, his only blood child. He and his wife had adopted three children after giving up on having their own. Then Heidi, the little miracle baby, appeared. Kurt held a special affection for his blonde, blue-eyed girl.

"Of course I will. I'll let Mom know so she can add us to next month's choir roster. I think we can be ready by then." I didn't want to delay too long. Kurt was noticeably failing.

Heidi, Kurt and I practiced our three parts. Sometimes he became so winded that he had to sit to sing, but we pressed on, his determination overcoming his infirmity.

On our appointed Sunday we positioned ourselves in the front pew. Kurt's wife sat next to her husband, holding a small tape recorder. We didn't attempt to scale the choir loft stairs, but stood on the floor. Kurt's complexion by now was pasty, colorless due to lack of oxygen, but he was eager to get this appearance in. We held our breath as he pushed himself up to stand and face the congregation. He was beaming. We began singing after my brief guitar lead in. *Some bright morning when this life is o'er, I'll fly away.* There were those words again. I felt sure Kurt knew exactly what he was singing this time.

We saw congregants wiping their eyes. Then they clapped and sang. Kurt's great harmonies, his triumph, brought a standing ovation, despite the church's policy about not erupting with applause in a worship service. No one fussed about it on this occasion. This joy was straight from heaven.

As Kurt's heart slowed, he descended into total dependence on his tiny wife, who could barely assist him at home by herself. She called me to come over and talk with them about Hospice.

Kurt was admitted to the House a few days later. Our music migrated to his room next to the nurses' station where he sat in a recliner, singing with me once again, with the aid of oxygen flowing freely into his lungs through a long, clear plastic tube. He had brought his manila folder of favorite songs and requested we sing one after the other, until I suggested he take a rest. He would have sung himself sick unless I stopped our sessions. I know the music distracted him, gave him hope in the darkness of his dying, lifted his spirits away from the irregular beating of his poor heart. Over the weeks we tore through that folder of music and then tackled an old red hymnal from church. He sang on.

And then he couldn't.

I entered his room on a bright winter day, ready to sing. He sat as usual in his recliner and welcomed me. I could see his eyes drooping with fatigue. His hands didn't reach for his music folder or the red hymnal on his chair-side table. His breathing had changed; now labored and staggering.

"I can't sing today," he said, huffing out those words as if he had run a marathon. Tears glazed over his weary eyes. I took a deep breath to keep my emotions in check. "I'll sing for you, if you want. You can put your head back and listen this time."

"Okay," he said, choking on that one word.

After I sang just two songs, he said he was tired, wanted to take a nap, then looked away from me, down at the floor. I think he couldn't bear having the music fill his ears without being able to join in as he always had. By now we were a duo, music buddies, close friends. He had found a voice he never knew he had.

With this new development, I hated telling him I was heading south in a couple of days, escaping the winter weather for a few weeks. I finally bent over his recliner and hugged him for a long time, kissed his cheek, then mentioned my trip. He looked up. Our eyes met. I stood motionless, unable to say goodbye. So instead I said I'd stay in touch, then collected my guitar, walked toward the door and turned back toward him. "I love you, Kurt," I said, waving, hurrying out the door. Once I was in the hallway and out of Kurt's earshot, I covered my face, leaned forward against the wall and cried out the grief that I had dammed up in my throat for a long time.

While I was in the South, I called Kurt's wife and daughter on a regular basis, keeping abreast of his condition. When they contacted *me*, I knew why they were calling. Kurt died peacefully. They tried to choose a date for his memorial service so I could participate, but the extended family was unable to accommodate that timeframe. I mourned not being present.

I am told that the church was packed for his service. The choir sang and lots of people got up to tell stories about big, burly Kurt.

But what really stuck in everyone's mind was the final music. A small tape recorder played Kurt, Heidi and me singing *I'll Fly Away*.

EVAN WILLIAMS

NO LIGHT

HIS WIFE'S SCREAMS RODE ON THE SUNBEAMS SHINING THROUGH
the gaps in the barn. He maintained his seat on a hay bale,
swigging cheap rye straight from a tall bottle. While inside their
hapless shack, critical seconds passed as the life-giving cord
snaked around the infant's neck. Only after intolerable annoyance
did the calloused hands of the sharecropper acquiesce to deliver
the baby girl.

At the bedside, he held his daughter, watching the mother's
blood spew from a worn-out womb. Locust-like it spread across
the dingy sheet, infuriating the man that the mattress would have
to be replaced.

Concern flashed across his wife's face, looking from her baby, to
him, questioning.

"You finally got your girl," he muttered.

"Beulah," she whispered. "Beulah," the relief of death's presence
erasing the worry etched in her weary brow. A half smile and she
faded away, the child's fate in his undecided hands.

A baby without a mother would be total nuisance, extra work on
a farm that already claimed everyone's waking hours. No kin around
to assist. A practical conclusion came easily to a mind unaccustomed
to options.

Seconds later two brothers rushed in from the cornfield, eyewitnesses to the writhing new sister in the father's grip.

Maybe she would have been better off not growing up without a mother, or never learning to read, judged too addled for school. Sentenced to a same-as-yesterday life, she survived as servant to father and five brothers. The object of the boys' fascination for her first years, she grew to become the center of their unwanted attention thereafter. As if her sole purpose was for their carnal desire, in turn.

At fifteen she stole away in the night, all her possessions fitting in a paper, grocery sack. In the last bit of moonlight before dawn, she rendezvoused with Bill Jakes at the edge of the north field. Ten years her senior, she didn't know any other eligible men. They met by accident weeks earlier when he came looking for his wandering milk cow. Eight farms removed from hers, she struck up a meeting place and time, halfway distant, shooing him off before her father and brothers came in for supper.

Bachelor life suited Bill fine, skittish around women and no longer waiting on his first kiss. But less than five minutes into their secret meeting, Beulah worked her plan, introducing him to the pleasures of the flesh. Now here he stood before her, shadows turning his dark hair to coal. She could feel her savior shaking when she took his hand.

"My uncle's car is parked along the edge of the road, on down by the creek. I reckoned nobody could hear it that far off."

Risking no further conversation, they walked a dim, white ribbon that cut between the trees. Minutes later, half-closing the car doors, they sped off, using the remainder of the night to cross the South Carolina state line, where a world of fifteen-year-olds had stood before the Justice of the Peace in Greenville, to be legally wed without consent of parents.

Life would be different. Maybe not so much better, but sometimes "different" was enough in a lackluster world.

***

"Take that squalling thing outside and be rid of it for good," barked Beulah, still carrying the name bestowed from her mother's favorite hymn—the only external link to her early years.

Wrapped in a tattered bathrobe peppered with food stains, she reigned from a shocking plaid couch, wallowed almost to floor level in its sagging middle. Though in her late thirties, the unkempt, brown hair and pasty indoor skin made her look half again her age. The only parts truly vibrant: grey eyes alive with rancor and a razor tongue that raced far ahead of a brain long ago deprived of oxygen.

The obscene racket came from the centermost occupant of a clowder of cats, swirling around a sizeable dark stain on the carpet of a cramped living room. One wide-open mouth wailed, while the group seemed intent on gleaning some measure of nutrition or flavor from the prominent spot, oddly shaped like the coastline of Greenland.

Unfazed by their feeding, Beulah's gaze did not waver from her true object of companionship, the second-hand television. Outdated and pushed beyond normal limits, it continued to provide constant reliability. The fact that the 'OFF' knob was unresponsive, presented no problem. It kept Beulah company from her permanent perch, where a tide of empty chip bags, popsicle sticks and Camel cigarette packs threatened to fill the void between the couch and the scorched coffee table. Blackened stubs overflowed from assorted ashtrays shoved one against another.

"But Beulah," the man began, raising his right hand to register objection to his wife's orders.

"No buts, Bill Jakes, or you'll pay hell. Now, do you want that?"

He couldn't control his dismay. "But we ain't had it two days. Let's give it some time. Maybe it'll hush on its own." He wanted her to look him in the eye, see his concern, but the jangling commercial for Palmolive dish detergent held more sway over her than he did.

"You heard me. Besides, how can I enjoy my programs with that little devil carrying on? I can't think with that noise." She grew louder.

He looked at her from under the brim of a greasy ball cap. "What about how you been saying you wanted one?"

"Well, guess I was wrong." She didn't like being forced into conversation with him, even if he did have sense enough to only talk during commercials. He knew, sure as rain on the roof that he better not open his yap while her shows were playing.

"So we went through all that trouble, and now it's come to getting rid of it right off the bat. Is that it?"

"That's about the size of it." Her answers were coming shorter and quicker.

Bill was a walking definition of "despondent," both in appearance and mental duress. More bone than meat, exaggerated by a tall frame, he trudged through the years humped at the shoulders, weighted by his life's lot. Sinewy hands and wrists extended way beyond the frayed cuffs of his second-hand shirt, picked out of the 'FREE' bin at The Good Samaritan—a local Baptist church's rummage basement. That's also where he got the cap, shielding his thinning scalp from days working in the sun, loading hay or picking pole beans from others' fields.

"Maybe it's hungry," he suggested. "Maybe that's why it's crying. Have you tried feeding it?"

"I ain't feeding it. You can. But why worry yourself when we're getting rid of it?"

Bill Jakes knew he couldn't take on feeding the young thing, at least not regular like. It took him working at any odd job that came along to keep them at their current level of poverty. No high school diploma and only a squeaky Huffy bicycle to get around meant menial work, mucking out stables and milking sheds, cleaning gas station bathrooms and any seasonal farm labor he could get.

The lack of vehicle made transporting necessities almost impossible. Finding a free, pink, Barbie backpack at the Good Samaritan didn't bring a smile to his face, but he saw the benefit to his dilemma. He gave no thought to the proportional disparity between the frame of a full-grown man and a young girls' backpack. He didn't even mind too much when Roy, the Shell station manager with nasty restrooms to clean, began calling him "Bill Barbie."

He couldn't afford to retaliate.

"You got your dollies in there Bill?" Roy would mock. But Bill went along with the bullying rather than explain most often he had it crammed with consumables for Beulah. That, or old magazines the small public library set out by the curb a few times each week. She liked to thumb through the pictures when reruns became too boring.

During his meager time off from wage earning, Bill could be seen fighting weeds and blackberry briers warring to engulf their house. Many days found him on the roof, applying whatever waterproof material he could add to the crazy-quilt pattern that barely kept out the rain.

His fondness for his childhood home motivated him to care for it, thankful for the familiarity as well as the excuse to get outside without the threat of her encroachment. He found enough peace around the property to sustain himself. Even Beulah's incessant abuse couldn't run him off.

Still in possession of a thin streak of optimism, he walked to their sad refrigerator and drew out the last sips of turning milk. Scooping up the quarrelsome newcomer, he held a teacup to the little mouth. No response. He tried again, adding encouraging words. "There, there. Try a little milk. It's good for you." No luck. Waiting a moment, he gave one last effort, accepting defeat.

Beulah didn't want to appear interested, but couldn't resist crushing him further. "See what I mean? It don't want to eat. It just wants to drive me crazy. Damn little devil. You satisfied now?"

Bill had the waif cradled in his flannelled elbow, but the volume did not decrease. "It ain't right to go and do something so cruel. What would folks think?"

"What folks, you fool? Ain't nobody around for half a mile. Thanks to that nitwit brain of yours we can't afford nothing but living in the sticks. Just an old shack ain't nobody else wanted. That's why your mama give it to you. Folks!" and she laughed.

He tried not to let on how much her laughing hurt him. Working slave hours with nothing but put downs for his trouble. She wasn't any smarter than him. Maybe not even half so smart. But smart enough to figure out how to watch TV all day while he did everything that needed to be done.

"Maybe it needs some kind of special food." His mind worked in slow increments, finally arriving at vague conclusions.

"Special food! Special food!" In her rage she almost rose up from the couch. "We're not about to go spending a penny on some special food for that good-for-nothing varmint. Have you forgot that we're saving to get a new TV and a prescription to the TV Guide?" The slothful fat of her face and neck had gone scarlet. "Well, have you?"

"I ain't forgot. But this is more important." He raised his head and puffed out his chest, determined he was in the right this time.

"Bill Jakes, now you listen to me, and listen to me good." She looked at him this time, her eyes squeezed almost shut, scowling her best mean face. "We was both raised up hard. Anything that didn't carry its weight, we got rid of."

Unable to grasp the ironic humor in the words coming from the hulk on the couch, he went silent. It was true, the growing up hard part. When the pet rabbit he rescued as a boy got into the family vegetable patch, Mama made him take it out to the woods and leave it. When it returned on its own, she threw it to the hound. Bill learned early that cruelty came with his world.

"Maybe somebody else'll want it."

"That ain't going to happen, not with the way the 'conomy is nowadays. Everbody's having a hard time just feeding themselves. That's all they want to talk about on the TV news. Now quit your whining and stalling. Be a man and do what has to be done." Her next words came with pauses between, as she sucked in air to scream at full volume. "Get—it—out—of—HERE!"

He felt nails piercing his head. Making a point lost all importance when being roared at by his wife. He could compromise his principles for some silence, already accustomed to paying the high price of just getting by.

"It ain't right," he whispered in defeat, staring at the blue eyes there in the crook of his arm. Maybe he aimed at a measure of forgiveness and understanding from one so purely innocent— voicing his objection, the helplessness of a submissive accomplice.

"The shovel's on the back porch, leaning near the door, from the other day when I got up that dead mouse off the kitchen floor." The finality in her words brought from him a deep sigh, as mismatched shoes moved to fetch the shovel.

"Bill." He paused, overcome with remorse, though also angry that she would stop him just shy of the door after he'd obviously agreed to carry out her wickedness. But what had he detected? A change in her tone? A lump came to his throat. The corners of his mouth started to turn up. Hope flickered, yet he dared not speak.

"If we'd a kept it, I was going to name it Junior—Bill Junior."

Bernie Brown

THE BEST SHOT

The clean harmony of The Drifters' "Up on the Roof" calmed Lance while he lay in bed in the half light of the radio's glow, his hands behind his head, staring at the ceiling. Between songs, Wolfman Jack growled out his philosophy like some wise old bear— mostly nonsense, Lance knew, but after midnight it made sense.

In Lance's head, the rhythmic smack of a dribbling basketball replaced the Drifters' harmony and Wolfman's growl. At practice tonight, he and Tommy, his best friend, had worked together as smoothly as if they were telepathic. Lance's passes shot straight into Tommy's hands like a magnet directed their course. Tommy's rebound angle directly mirrored the angle from which Lance shot. Lance and Tommy always worked well together, but tonight they had been on fire. Here's hoping they could keep that fire burning tomorrow night at the Benton game.

He and Tommy had been playing together since Lance's dad mounted a hoop on the garage when Lance was seven. They had played so continuously that Lance had lost count how many times the net had been replaced. Sometime in all those basketball years, a plan evolved in which they would both play basketball at the State University of Iowa in Iowa City. Tommy wanted it. Tommy's dad wanted it. Lance's dad hadn't been good enough for college ball, so he wanted it. Heck, the whole town of Carlton took it as an accomplished fact when they were just sophomores.

Not once had it occurred to Lance to question the plan. Not until a nameless longing bounced around in Lance's chest like a basketball on the loose. Lance refused to chase it down.

With a click, Lance silenced Wolfman, rolled over and waited for sleep. Somewhere in that gray place between waking and sleeping, when his defenses were down, the elusive desire revealed itself. He sat up, awake and energized, recognizing the longing for what it was, and knew what he wanted.

***

Lance leaned against the wall by the school counselor's office, one knee bent, his foot on the wall. He clutched his books before him with both hands, every few minutes tilting the books sideways to check his watch. He knew Mr. Slater showed up right before the bell every morning, the kids joked about how close he cut it.

At last the counselor appeared around the corner, taking his sweet time, stopping at the office to pick up his mail. Lance willed him to move faster.

When he was within a few feet, Lance spoke up. "I need to talk to you." Lance could smell his soap. He had probably finished shaving just minutes ago.

Mr. Slater reached his door, fished in his pocket for the key, and answered as he unlocked his office. "Sure, Lance. Now?"

"I've got study hall third. Can you give me a pass?"

Mr. Slater scribbled a pass. Lance flew down the hall and skated in to English just as the bell rang and Mrs. Hamilton closed the door. English and Chemistry passed at a snail's pace. At last he was seated in the counselor's office, one of the few places in the school where the kids were provided an upholstered chair. In spite of that, Lance couldn't get comfortable. He crossed his right ankle on his left knee. Then he reversed the position. Then he put both feet flat on the floor.

Mr. Slater shut the door, giving the small, messy office a tempting intimacy that invited secrets. He sat down with the sigh of a heavy man. Lance liked Mr. Slater. He was big and comfortable. When he yelled at the kids to stop running in the halls, they did. "What's up, Lance?" he said, looking Lance straight in the eye, and fiddling with his pen.

"I've been thinking about after graduation."

"Never too soon."

Lance shifted again. He couldn't look at Mr. Slater when he talked. "Well, I don't know where I got this idea, but I'm thinking about the Air Force Academy." Lance felt foolish, like he was giving voice to some wild scheme. He feared any kind of extreme reaction from Slater.

Mr. Slater had no reaction. He just said, "Interesting," and waited for Lance to go on.

"What do you think? Is it possible? I mean, how do I go about it? I haven't said anything to my parents. My dad wants me to go to Iowa City. I don't know how to tell him. To ask him." As Lance gave voice to his questions, to the obstacles he anticipated, he became more resolute and raised his head to look the counselor in the eye. He stopped fidgeting.

"Let's take it a step at a time."

***

The last bell finally put an end to the interminable day. Lance couldn't wait to talk to Tommy about his plan while they sat together on the team bus to Benton. They usually talked about college basketball or their parents or girls or just slept. Ignoring the horseplay of his pent-up team mates, Lance rattled on to Tommy about the academy, how he had to write to the governor and send an essay. He failed to notice that the set of Tommy's mouth grew more and more tense. At last Lance paused for breath.

"Where?" Tommy asked with a nasty edge to his voice, like Lance had said he wanted to go to college on the moon. "What made you think of that?" Tommy's dismissive response surprised Lance at first, and then he realized his own disregard for Tommy's feelings. With this news, Lance had bailed on the plans they'd made long ago. Silence descended between them like a bad smell.

At last Tommy said something. "I thought we were going to Iowa City."

"You know that's mostly my dad that wants that."

"Well, sorr-ee." Tommy acted like this was news to him.

Lance had assumed Tommy would be happy for him. Yeah, like expecting someone to smile after you hit him upside the head. Lance felt like the gum on the bottom side of the bleachers. Although he and Tommy shared a seat, a distance the size of a basketball court stretched between them.

During the game, the tension between the two threw them off their timing, their aim, their mutual ESP. Lance was under the backboard looking at Tommy to feed him the ball. Tommy hesitated a moment too long, and the Benton guard stepped out and grabbed the ball, going for a fast break. Stuff like that never happened generally, but repeated itself in this forsaken game. The coach was baffled, the rest of the team was thrown off by Tommy and Lance's behavior, and the whole evening was a painful experience. Carlton won by a margin of five points, but that was no satisfaction since Benton was a purely mediocre team.

After the game, Coach came in the locker room with a face like thunder. "What the hell happened out there? Lance? Tommy? I never saw you two foul up like that. I don't know what's going on between you, but if you don't settle it, I'll put you both on the bench." He scuffed his foot like a five-year-old and the whole team stared at the floor, ashamed.

On the bus home, surrounded by the night-darkened glass of the windows, seated in the dirty plastic seats that made sucking sounds when he moved around and smelled of sweat, Lance sat five rows behind Tommy. Lance braced his knees against the seat in front of him, crossed his arms on them and put his head down, feigning sleep. The other players avoided him like they'd catch whatever had jinxed his game.

***

The interminable bus ride finally brought the team back to town. Lance cut through all the back yards to his house where he took the stairs to his room two at a time. He crawled into bed and stared at the ceiling, waiting for the comfort of The Drifters' harmony or Wolfman's words. Lance accepted that he'd alienated

Tommy. Even though Tommy's defection pained Lance, it didn't change his mind. He had passed one hurdle, however poor his timing, and it was time to face the next one. He steeled himself for his dad's reaction.

**

On Sunday afternoon, Lance approached his dad at the kitchen table. Toaster parts littered the table top as if the device had exploded. His dad poked at the toaster's exposed wiring with his screwdriver, his brow furrowed. Silently, Lance took the chair opposite him, staring at the top of his dad's head. Lance's hands were as damp as his mouth was dry.

Easing into the subject, Lance began. "Dad, you know how you always wanted me to go to Iowa City?" He mustered his courage as he waited for his dad's response.

His dad kept tinkering. The screwdriver made little clicking sounds as it scraped the edges of the small appliance. "Yeah?" his dad grunted, his attention still on the wiring.

This was going to be even harder than Lance thought. Clearly, his dad hadn't a clue that he wanted something else. "Well, you see, I've been talking to Mr. Slater—he's the school counselor . . ."

His dad interrupted. "He's not trying to get you to go out of state is he? Not Illinois." He was going off on totally the wrong tack. His dad hated Illinois basketball.

Lance had to say it straight out. "Dad, I want to go to the Air Force Academy in Colorado." His brow broke out in a sweat. His armpits got sticky.

His dad's mouth opened to a perfect O, like a cartoon character. Under any other circumstances, Lance would have laughed. His dad put down his screwdriver and stared at him. Lance feared a tirade, but none came. Instead, his dad's eyes got misty, and his voice turned soft.

"Colorado? The Air Force? Where you'd get that idea, son?"

Lance explained about his talks with the counselor.

His dad ran the back of his hand over his eyes. "My cousin Randall was in the Army Air Corps. That's all there used to be. He was a flyer in the war. Killed at Normandy. He was a real hero.

We were close growing up." The mist of memory took his dad away for a few moments. A look of grief and pain flickered over his face, and Lance had to look away.

Then his dad straightened, "That's a fine idea, son. You'd do us proud to go there." Then he did something he never did, he reached across the table and covered Lance's hand with his own warm, rough one. He left it there a moment, and it calmed Lance, reassured him, and buoyed him up. The effect stayed with him even after his dad withdrew his hand to pick up his screwdriver.

***

His application to the Air Force Academy preoccupied Lance the next few weeks. He and Mr. Slater huddled in the counseling office over the letter to Governor Hazlitt. "Now is not the time to be modest, Lance," the counselor said.

Mr. Slater left for a few minutes, and Lance made a start. He summarized his academic and athletic performance and then he got in the swing of it. "I want very much to attend the Air Force Academy to honor my dad's cousin, a pilot who died in the Normandy Invasion." He had first thought of saying that just to influence the governor emotionally, but the more he thought about it, the more his desire became linked to that family history. And then he was done. He read it over as Mr. Slater came back.

Mr. Slater read it, too, and said, "I didn't know this about your relative."

"My dad just told me about it."

"Well, I'm sure that will make a difference," Mr. Slater said. He went on, "I hope this clinches an interview for you, Lance."

Lance looked up. Time stopped. Lance's hopes fell out the bottom of his chest. He didn't know about any interview. "Uh, interview?"

"We talked about it. The governor invites you to be interviewed, you talk to him, and he decides if he'll give you an appointment to the academy. That's the way it works."

Lance felt his head nodding agreement, but no agreement existed inside him, only a certainty that he couldn't possibly talk to the governor. He would feel so outclassed, like playing ball against a pro team. Or what if he screwed up like the time he flubbed that presentation in English? Lance ran his hand through his hair a couple of times.

Mr. Slater took a look at his watch, said he had an appointment and he'd see Lance tomorrow.

***

Lance sat in his car in the school parking lot taking deep breaths. There went his dream, sudden death by interview. Persevering after Tommy's rejection and enlisting his dad's support had summoned all the courage Lance possessed. The well was dry.

Lance drove home slowly, as if the car was weighed down as heavily as his heart. In the house, his mom looked at him and Lance knew she had read his mind, the way she could when he was a little kid. He didn't speak, just went to his room and shut the door.

He turned on the radio, flopped on his bed, and loathed himself in as many ways as he good devise. He lost track of how long he lay there until a knock made him focus. "Yeah?"

"Lance, let me talk to you." It was his dad.

Lance sat up and straightened his hair with his hands. "Come on in."

His dad came in, pulled out the chair by the desk, and sat on it facing Lance, "What's wrong here? Your mom said you're upset. Is it the academy?"

Lance told him about Slater springing the interview on him. "He says he told me about it before, but I swear, I would have remembered." He ran his hands through his hair again, he just couldn't stop doing that. His cheeks burned when he said, "Man, Dad, I just can't go talk to the governor. He's like," Lance searched for the right words, but found none, "The Governor, for Pete's sake."

Lance could see his dad taking it in, sorting it out, and then – Lance least expected this – his dad leaned on the back two chair legs and let out a hoot. And then another one. He laughed and laughed.

Lance stared at him as if he'd gone mad.

Finally, his dad got control, tilted the chair forward on all four legs and said, "Is that all?"

"Isn't that enough?"

"I thought they'd turned you down flat or something."

Lance had hoped for more sympathy.

His dad went on. "Of course you can talk to the governor. He's just a man like me or Mr. Slater."

Lance started to run his hands through his hair, and then stopped.

"If it helps, we could practice being interviewed."

A brave ray of light penetrated Lance's gloom.

***

So Mr. Slater sent the letter, and every evening after supper Lance and his dad practiced interviewing.

"When was the Air Force Academy founded?"

"Why do you want to attend the academy?"

"What importance do athletics play in your life?"

Answers emerged like reluctant players at first, clumsy and hesitant. With practice, Lance no longer stammered when he responded. He smiled, he elaborated, he used his hands to make a particularly salient observation. Soon, he was bursting with impatience to make the governor's acquaintance.

He didn't have to wait long.

***

On an unseasonably hot day in April, Lance and his dad set out for Des Moines and the capitol building in his dad's new '63 Chevy. To keep his white shirt fresh for the interview, Lance hung it in the backseat. It looked like a third, more grown-up body in the car, waiting for Lance to inhabit it.

While his dad drove, Lance rested his arm on the open window, tapping his fingers on the rim. He fiddled with the radio, trying to find just the right music to match his feelings of impatience and dread.

Once, his dad asked him if he wanted to review any of the questions, but Lance shook his head. A few times a subversive thought slipped past Lance's carefully guarded confidence. The thought told him, *Turn around and head home, you fool.* Each time Lance slapped it down and shored up his defenses.

Only when the gold-domed Capitol rose before him, did Lance's self-absorption give way to humbling amazement. A now-or-never resolution replaced wavering doubt. He grabbed his dress shirt from the back and stood just outside the parked car as he slipped it on over his tee shirt, like putting on a game uniform. His dad waited in the car. When Lance was ready, his dad got out, helped him with his tie, and shook his hand. "Give it your best shot, son."

***

Lance was glad to see the governor wore shirt sleeves, too. In fact, they were dressed almost exactly alike. Lance felt like he and this man were the only two people in the world, that only this moment existed in time. The office windows were open and the distant sounds of traffic and birdsong reminded him that there was, indeed, other life going on out there.

They shook hands and sat down; and, as his dad had suggested, Lance asked the governor where he was from. He watched as the politician could not resist talking about himself, which he did for about thirty minutes.

As if coming to an afterthought, the governor began his questions for Lance. Several were identical to his dad's mock interview questions, so that Lance's answers came readily. Just as Lance was really warming to his task, the governor rose and smiled. "I've got a lunch meeting, so I'll have to close, but I really enjoyed talking to you, Lance You'll be hearing from me soon." And it was over.

Lance's legs propelled him down the marble corridors and staircase, but his head felt detached, surreal. He couldn't mentally connect with the fact that the interview was over and he had survived, actually triumphed. No matter what happened now, this felt like success. He had lost the support of his best friend, risked the love and respect of his father, and conquered his fear of personal interaction with the state's most prestigious leader. But he had pulled it off.

When he reached the grass outside he couldn't contain a war whoop that sailed up to the trees and frightened the birds. He felt like Wilt Chamberlain and Bob Cousy rolled into one. Lance's legs raised him off the ground in a jump shot sans ball, while Lance made a swish sound to accompany it. His dad leaned against the car, arms crossed, a grin the size of Texas on his face.

Lance took off his tie, threw it in the back seat, and told his dad all about the interview, elaborating on the governor's own athletic career. He babbled all through lunch at McDonald's while his dad just nodded and wore that goofy grin that was new to him.

In McDonald's parking lot after lunch, Lance's dad asked him if he wanted to drive home. Lance took the wheel, turned on the radio, and pulled onto the highway. As the white center line of Interstate 80 unfurled before him, the deejay introduced the next song. "Let's give a listen to a hit from a few years ago, one of my personal favorites. Here are the Drifters with 'This Magic Moment' from 1960."

Lance turned up the volume, cranked down his window, and sang along as he and his dad cruised back home.

Heath Towson

THE GLASS KEYS

Glancing down at the clock on my computer, I noticed that it was 10:30 p.m. The earth cloaked in darkness, tonight was another late one in tax season. While most in Asheville were settled in watching TV or lying still in their beds, we at Ketch and Sells Public Accountants kept the midnight flame burning. The coffee maker brewed up another pot to fuel new hires trying to prove themselves. I was one of those new hires, arriving as early as possible and staying as late as our senior partner, Mr. Boris. A self-described workaholic like most accountants, he could be beat in the morning by almost no one, nor could any stay quite as late.

Ketch and Sells was housed in a repurposed knitting mill, a ghost of Asheville's past and a victim of our over gentrified downtown. Because of the building's historic nature, it could be somewhat eerie. Its expansive hallways, lined in creaky pine boards, thick with layers of varnish. Large windows that ran floor to ceiling would echo the howls of winter wind, culminating in a lonely feeling late at night. Mr. Boris' office was across the main floor from my desk. Peering over my cubicle, his office was still aglow, adding machine chattering away. I had gotten to know him fairly well as he had assigned me to work on several of his complicated tax returns. He was unhappy with the work of my cubicle neighbor, Thomas Proper and asked that I work with him. Still getting to know everyone at the firm, I would come to find out that Thomas Proper held a dark secret.

Thomas Proper was a very interesting person. He was probably several years older than me, maybe in his late twenties. He did not arrive until nearly nine in the morning and then would emerge from his slow moving, elderly Toyota Camry with a back pack and plaid print lunch box. I would see him stuff his large lunch box in the fridge and then make his way over to his cubicle. He would usually greet me with "hey there, how's it going," or something of that nature. He was one of these people that was entirely over qualified for everything, yet had never really done anything with their lives. He told me one day while working together, that he had passed the BAR exam to become a lawyer, worked for a law office and even passed the CPA exam.

Despite all of these qualifications, Thomas still lived at home with his parents. He drove their hand-me-down car and wore his father's old suits, which appeared to be left over from the 1980s judging by their dated style and old fashioned cut. I guessed from his description of his parents, they were older and that he probably came from "old money", leading a cushy life. I'm sure his mom still packed his lunch.

Thomas came over to my cubicle with a file from Mr. Boris and flashed an awkward smile in my direction.

"Hi, Thomas, what's up man?" I asked.

"Heeey, Jeff, do you have a minute to help me look over this file? I've been over it several times, but I can't seem to get the numbers to balance."

"I'm a little busy working on a return that has to get out this afternoon, but if you want to leave it here, I can take a look through it later and meet up with you?"

"Sure, that will work" he said with an annoyed sigh as he hoisted the large brown accordion file onto my desk. It looked like it took all his strength to lift as he was a mousy, little man. He flashed a beady eyed look my way, smiled wryly and walked slowly back to his desk.

As the afternoon began to wind down and I had overcome the stupor of my post lunch malaise, I decided to take a look into the file that Thomas had set at the edge of my desk earlier. The setting sun cast a direct beam on an old looking envelope stuffed in the edge of the file. Most of our clients gave us all kinds of financial information to prepare their return like letters, or shoeboxes full of receipts for their groceries from 1987. I pulled the letter out of the file along with the rest of the financial statements and began to examine them. The letter was not addressed to the client though; it was addressed to Thomas.

The seal on the envelope was broken, and, oddly, it was an old fashioned wax seal. The envelope looked yellowed with age and had the address typed on it, obviously done with a typewriter. Since the seal was broken, I decided to read the letter as it might contain correspondence with Thomas and the client. I began to read the letter and could not believe what I was seeing.

January 4, 1939

Dear Mr. Proper,

Thank you for writing to inquire about our typewriter ribbons. For the model typewriter you requested (Underwood No. 5 Typewriter) we still carry a variety of ribbons despite the age of this model. Please send a self-addressed envelope with five stamps for payment to the following address:

Non-Smut Carbon Manufacturing Company, Inc.
49 Mohawk St.
Buffalo, New York

If you find you need further assistance, please dial us at Cleveland 2565 in the New York area. Good-luck on your further typewriter purchases and thank you for contacting us.

Sincerely,
Leo Winans

How was it possible that Thomas could have seemingly reached back in time to inquire about typewriter ribbons for some old typewriter? I decided to do an Internet search to see when this typewriter had been made. With fingers quickly gliding across my keyboard, I found that model typewriter had not been made since the early 1900s! The Non-Smut manufacturing company had gone out of business shortly after World War II. Was this some kind of joke or faux letter that Thomas had written? Just as I was about to get to work preparing the file, Thomas appeared at the side of my desk with a worried look on his face.

"Hey, Jeff, can I grab that letter? It wasn't supposed to make it in with the client's file. I'm terribly sorry about that."

"Sure, Tom, no worries. Here you go."

"It's Thomas, and thank you. Awfully sorry. Just an old letter from my uncle."

He stuffed the letter under his arm and hurried back to his desk. I couldn't help but note his stranger-than-usual behavior regarding the letter.

The next day, Thomas was out sick. Despite his daily tardiness, he seemingly never missed work. He was a creature of habit and even wore the same green plaid shirt every Friday. I went up to the front of the office to check my mail box, and noticed a medium sized carton at the front desk for Thomas. Our secretary, June, a tall, buxom redhead with long brightly colored nails greeted me. She always had a tight, form-fitting dress, several rings on each finger and six inch heels, to add to her already domineering stature. Despite the dullness of accounting, this had to be one of the best parts of my day.

"Hey, honey, will you take this to Thomas' desk? He's been shipping his packages here again," she said annoyed. Most of the administrative ladies did not like Thomas.

"Sure. You got it, June!" I said in my usual overexcited tone.

"Thanks, dear. You're the best!"

I heaved the box from the front counter, where June flashed a flirty look my way, and carried it to Thomas' desk. As I set it down, I heard some kind of bell go off inside. Whatever was in the box, it weighed a ton. The cardboard had an odor of an older person's home, which typically contain a smell of musty basement and urine. As the day passed, the thought of the letter from the day before and this odd package arriving at Thomas' desk started to gnaw at me.

The next morning, Thomas slowly sauntered to his desk around 9:05am. As soon as he caught sight of the package, his pace increased to a fast trot. He leaned around the edge of my cubicle and exclaimed:

"Jeff, it's here! Come take a look!" he squealed.

"What's here, Thomas?" I replied over the wall of my cubicle.

"My new Royal Series 90 typewriter!"

"Okay, just give me a sec," I muttered as I heaved my weary bones from the flattened foam of my desk chair.

There, sitting on Thomas' desk was an ornate, old typewriter, probably from the 1920s. The case of the machine was flanked with nickel-plated hardware that gleamed in the fluorescent lighting. In the middle of the machine was emblazoned "Royal" in gold, outlined in white pinstriping. The glass covered keys shone in their own way. It was rather handsome looking.

"Have you ever seen one like this before?" Thomas exclaimed.

"No, I can't say that I have. Where do you get something like this?"

"From eBay of course," he replied snarkily. "It's a real beauty!"

"What do you plan to do with it?" I replied, somewhat baffled.

"Well! I plan to type on it! Can't let a gorgeous machine like this go to waste!"

"Do you write?"

"You could say I use these typewriters to . . . communicate," he said in an ominous tone. "I need to get back to work," he snapped. "Just wanted to show you."

As four o'clock rolled around, I could tell that I was going to need to stay late again. Mr. Boris had come by my desk to drop off several bloated accordion files that needed to be reviewed before the next day.

At around 4:59, I heard Thomas noisily packing his back pack and slamming the screen of his laptop computer in a hurry. He then peered around the edge of my cubicle to say something.

"Hey, Jeff, sorry I can't help you with the return Mr. Boris assigned us this afternoon. I really need to get to the post office and mail a couple of bills."

"No worries, brotha, we'll catch you tomorrow." I sighed in exhaustion.

"Thanks, man!" he exclaimed like a school boy. "Can you help me carry my typewriter out to the car tomorrow? I just don't want to take a risk dropping it in the parking lot. You are welcome to come to dinner at my house if you like? Mom is making baked macaroni and cheese!"

"All right, sure. Can't say no to a free meal! See you then, man."

As weird as Thomas and his family seemed, it was better than going home to my tiny West Asheville apartment and eating SpaghettiOs. Thomas walked out at his usual snail's pace, carrying a stack of envelopes clutched tightly in his tiny hands. They were old fashioned looking letter sized envelopes with gloss red wax seals on them. Rather fancy for a bill that he was supposedly mailing. I figured maybe I would gain an insight on his behavior after eating dinner with his family.

After dinner and a quick beer with our office manager Nick, we headed back for a long night of reviewing some returns. Nick was a stocky, middle-aged Pennsylvanian who joked with and looked after everyone. It took some of the edge off the complexity of work that we did during the day. He had noticed that Thomas was pretty odd too.

"Jeff, I noticed you have been working with Thomas a lot. How's that going? You know ol' Boris has his doubts about the little guy," Nick asked.

"Eh, it's all right. He seems to work pretty slowly, but he's all right. Kind of strange though. Did you know Thomas is really into typewriters?"

"What the hell does he want one of those for? Big heavy things that you practically have to punch to get them to spit out a letter! The only reason I took typing in school was to pick up chicks," he replied in his usual gruff manner.

"Who knows, man . . . who knows . . ." I said as my words trailed off into the roar of a large diesel truck passing us on the street.

I was glad Nick was here; the building seemed to be extra spooky at night. After all, misery loves company. We trudged up the steps to the back door and exchanged high fives before returning to our respective desks.

"I'll stop by your desk later and check on you, bro," said Nick. He knew how much pressure I was under.

"Thanks, man, I'd appreciate that. These returns are absolutely killer."

Nick gave me a reassuring wink and walked back to his office at the far corner of the building.

When I rounded the corner where Thomas' desk was, I saw the black paint of his new Royal typewriter gleaming in the minimal light of the office. Mr. Boris' adding machine was whirring away in the distance. As I sat down to boot up my computer, I started to hear a light clicking from Thomas' cubicle. I figured it was just my exhaustion and rubbed my eyes as my computer came to life. Mr. Boris emerged from his office to take a break, pacing up and down the hall. He often would check through the recycling cans of employees and make sure they weren't filling them up with excess papers that could be put in the trash instead. He was so miserly, he did not want to pay the extra cost for the recycling truck to come by.

As Mr. Boris rifled through various employees' recycle bins, I heard him let out a gruff bark. Soon after, the click of his leather-bottom loafers approached my desk. He had been mumbling something about old letters and "what the hell are these?"

"Jeff, do you know anything about some letters from Thomas to a Ms. Lena Gerhardt? They have some fancy wax seals on the envelope and he keeps putting them in the recycling bin when he needs to put them in the trash. Is this his girlfriend? Why is he writing these at work?"

"Well . . . uh . . . I can take a look at them and see?"

"Hmmphh, yeah, take a look at these and see what this is. He shouldn't be doing this at work. How's he doing?"

"Well, he seems to be a little behind, but he has helped me on some projects."

"Ah, well! All right. Look at those letters, tell me about them and then finish out these last couple of files."

"Sure, Mr. Boris. Will do."

He walked off in a huff back to his office, his footsteps scuffing against the uneven pine floor and echoing off the tall cement columns. As I spread the letters across my desk to look over, I heard the clicking and clacking again from Thomas' desk beside me. I peered over the top of the desk and saw nothing but his large Royal typewriter sitting there. I started to scan the letter and saw the date was 1939 again. This just didn't seem to make sense. Click. Tick tick tick. Tick tick tick came from Thomas' desk. Curious about his machine, I picked up a piece of paper and decided to test it out.

When I arrived at Thomas' desk, my movement bumped the mouse of his computer, awakening the screen. Strangely, he had left an obituary up for Nelson Baker. After scrolling down the screen, I noticed that Nelson was a civil engineer from Arkansas who died in the 1940s.

I grabbed a piece of paper from under his desk and slipped it into the rollers of the machine. Before I could strike a key, the machine began to type on its own! Then, after it finished typing a sentence, the bell rang, signaling that the carriage needed to be pushed back. The message on the piece of paper said:

THOMAS IS IN GREAT DANGER. TELL HIM NOT TO FOOL WITH LENA ANYMORE. EDWIN IS VERY UNHAPPY.
–NELSON

I was stunned at what I was seeing from this old machine. It didn't seem to be typing anymore, so I looked around Thomas' desk for more clues. I looked around the typewriter and noticed some etching towards the base of the machine. It had the name Nelson Baker etched into the side of it! The machine must have belonged to him a long time ago. Maybe Thomas had some odd fascination with him? From the obituary, it seemed like he was a pretty normal guy. Besides being a civil engineer, it showed that he also was a Sunday school teacher in Little Rock, Arkansas. My heart raced as I looked down again at the page and wondered if I should warn Thomas. I figured I was imagining all of this and snatched the paper from the machine and crumpled it up in the garbage.

I went back to the letters at my desk to see what they said. They were from Thomas to a Mrs. Lena Gerhardt, dated 1939. The first letter read:

Thomas Proper
100 Blue Moon Lane,
Asheville, NC
January 8th, 1939

Dear Thomas,
   I absolutely adored the last bit of love poetry you sent my way. It was divine and made my southern heart swoon with delight. Something you wrote about how the Spanish moss sways with a soft whisper of love that is the breeze. Any who, I hope I get to meet you soon. This whole being in love through the mail is something different, but gives me a nice reprieve from my jealous husband. He found one of your letters the other day and it absolutely drove him mad! You should have seen the way he kicked over the mailbox and stormed off the porch. Take care of yourself and write soon.

        Yours,
        -Lena

The year was 2014 for crying out loud! How could he be writing back in time to these people? First these letters from a woman who should be long since dead, then a typewriter on his desk typing out warnings to me? I ran down the hall to Nick's office to show him the letters that Mr. Boris had thrown on my desk. It looked like whatever I may learn during dinner with Thomas and his family would prove to be very enlightening.

When I arrived at Nick's office, he looked up with concern. Out of breath, I stammered:

"Nick, Nick, you've got to see this. This typewriter on Thomas' desk is typing all on its own!"

"What are you talking about, bro? Was there something special in that beer you had?"

"No! Come with me! You've got to see this. Thomas is into some weird stuff, and it looks like he might be in trouble!"

"Well . . . all right, man. Whatever you say. Let's go take a look."

Nick tried to keep up with me as I dashed back to Thomas' desk. I showed him all of the strange things like the obituary and the engraving on the side of the typewriter. I pulled the crumpled page that contained the warning from Nelson out of my trash can and showed it to him. We put a piece of paper into the typewriter and . . . nothing. Just like in all of the classic movies, it wouldn't type for me.

"Look, man, I know you've been under a lot of stress and this definitely seems weird, but I think you need to go home and get some rest. I have a meeting with Thomas tomorrow to discuss projects and files he is working on. Why don't you see if you can take a look through that back pack he is always carrying for some more clues," said Nick.

"I swear! It was typing. Ah! Oh well. You're probably right. I need some rest. I'll catch you in the morning."

"Take it easy, bro. We'll see you tomorrow."

The next day, I sat waiting neurotically at my desk for Thomas to arrive. At exactly 9:05 a.m., he appeared through the door with his back pack and plaid print lunch box. He sat down slowly at his desk and gave me a hello nod. Nick came by and asked Thomas if he was ready for his work flow meeting. As the two of them walked off, Nick gave me a quick wink.

As soon as Nick and Thomas left, I crept around Thomas' desk and unzipped his back pack. Inside were glass covered typewriter keys cut off many machines. I had always noticed that he "jingled" when he walked. There were some more crumpled up letters and some old typewriter parts like ribbons and correction tape. At the bottom of the pack, was an old leather-bound book of love poems with dried flowers pressed into it. I opened the book to the inside cover and inscribed was "To my dear Thomas, Love Lena." So it looked like Thomas had some kind of magical powers with typewriters and was having a love affair across dimensions. Interesting!

After the day reached its end, dragging by with all of its might, it was finally time to take the typewriter to Thomas' house.

"Hey, Jeff, you ready to go, man?" said Thomas.

"Sure, dude, you ready?"

"Yes. Please lift the typewriter carefully and follow me to my car."

I heaved the cast iron beast off his desk and followed him slowly to his car. Thomas, despite his pace, was one of these people who had a bounce to their walk, which slightly annoyed me. I placed the typewriter carefully into his musty back seat and off we went.

"Do you just want to follow me to my parents' house?" he said.

"Sure, that works fine for me. I need to split and come back to the office anyway."

"Okay, that will be fine. I have some things I need to catch up on tonight," Thomas said mysteriously.

I leapt into my pickup truck and followed him back to his parents' house. We were headed toward Biltmore Forest, an elite neighborhood in Asheville of stale, old wealth. Its gated confines, a statement of days gone by, were filled with large Tudor style homes.

As we pulled into his cobblestone driveway, I could see through leaded pane windows, a dimly lit dining room where his parents were doddering about. Thomas slid over the threshold of his car door like an old man and motioned for me to come and get the typewriter. I slid down cautiously from the elevation of my pickup truck, my boots touching the cobblestone driveway. I pulled the typewriter from his elderly Camry and we proceeded down the rhododendron-lined path to a mighty oak front door. Thomas clasped the ornate, wrought iron door knob between his nimble fingers and heaved at the door with all his might. Once we entered the foyer of the house, he instructed me to put the typewriter down on an Edwardian style table next to the door.

"We'll put it here for now, until Mom makes me take it back up to my room," said Thomas with his usual air of presumption. "Come this way. Mom texted me that dinner is hot on the table!"

"Cool, sounds good, man. I'm starved!"

We proceeded into the formal dining room where, inexplicably, the family ate every night. My assumption that he had come from old money was proving to be true.

When we arrived in the kitchen, his parents greeted me with a hearty "Hello!" His father was wearing a navy blazer with brass buttons and a crest on the front that said Biltmore Forest Country Club. His mother was wearing a white and blue striped sweater that looked very nautical with khaki pants and canvas sneakers. They looked like an old pair that had just returned from a trip to their yacht.

"Jeff, please sit down here and we will serve you. Nice of you to help Thomas bring home his typewriter. I don't know why he is still collecting the damn things when you kids are all on your cell phones and iPads all day. He's got a whole bloody room full of them!" said Mr. Proper.

"Dad! Just stop it, okay?" whined Thomas. "I love them and they speak to me."

"He's always going on about how they speak to him," said Mrs. Proper. "We were so glad when computers came along so we didn't have to drag one of those things out just to write a letter to a friend."

"He'll have to take you up to his room later and show them to you. He's got shelves full of them," said Thomas' father in the typical way that parents ask you to show belongings you don't really want to.

"Jeff, do you want to go up and see my typewriter collection after dinner?" asked Thomas with chipper enthusiasm.

"Uh, sure man," I stammered.

Dinner seemed fairly normal. It was a traditional Southern meal of baked macaroni, cooked apples and vegetables. After dinner, we went into the parlor where we sat on sunken, musty, patterned furniture. No meal in the South with guests would be complete without dessert and coffee to accompany strained conversation.

We had just finished dessert when Thomas impatiently asked me to go upstairs to his room and see his typewriter collection. I thanked his parents for dinner and followed the pouty little man to his room. It was like I was hanging out with a friend from fourth grade all over again. We proceeded up the old wooden stairs that creaked with each tread. The walls were flanked by large, brass trimmed wooden rails that ran all the way to the top. Arriving at the top of the stairs, we reached Thomas' room. It had a large wooden door with a maroon colored "T" stenciled on the outside in old English script.

As we entered the room, I saw around a dozen or more typewriters lined up on a wide, built-in shelf. They were all lit by individual lights and had manila envelopes below each of them with papers squeezed tightly in each folder.

"This is where it all happens," said Thomas in an eerie distant way. "One of my other typewriters told me about your communication with Nelson, how he wrote to you on the Royal. He's upset because I am communicating via typewriter with a man's wife. We've fallen in love."

"Thomas, I uh . . . isn't this a bad idea to be communicating with these ghosts? Can they harm you? Why do you have all of those typewriter keys in your back pack?"

"Oh, you saw the glass keys did you? I have to cut them from the typewriter for them to stop communicating with me! The ghost can no longer press the keys of the typewriter thus killing the machine. I keep several on the dead shelf up there," he said, pointing upward.

"Are Edwin and Lena the man and wife you speak of?"

"Yes, Lena and I are in love. Edwin goes raving mad when he sees me write to her. I've cut the keys from his typewriter and sold them for jewelry. This has angered him even more!"

"What if he hurts you?"

"What could he possibly do? You see all of these machines? These envelopes contain all of the letters I have written their owners. Sometimes they leave a letter in the case or put their name on the side of the machine. I research their personal information and communicate with them through the typewriter.

Out of the corner of my eye, I could see one of the dead typewriters moving toward the edge of the shelf it was perched precariously on. All of a sudden, the typewriters in the room started going wild. Their bells were ringing and keys clacking away, typing different messages on the paper pressed against their platens.

"Thomas! What's happening?" I exclaimed.

"I don't know! Stop! Stop I say!" he said.

The machines kept on typing like they were possessed by the energy of a large electrical storm. I looked away for a moment to see what they were writing and the next thing I knew, there was a large crash! Thomas let out a little whimper. I could see that a large cast iron type writer had fallen from the shelf and hit him on the head! I called for his parents and an ambulance. On the floor next to the dead machine that had fallen on Thomas, lay a piece of paper that had floated down from above:

DON'T MESS WITH MY WOMAN! I TOLD YOU ONCE AND NOW YOU WILL PAY! –EDWIN

After that fateful night, things seemed odd around the office. Thomas hadn't shown up for several days, and I couldn't get in contact with his parents. Finally, word passed to us that Thomas had died from the trauma of the machine falling on his head. The past few days had been an unbelievable whirlwind.

A week later, a rough, crumpled cardboard box arrived for me at the office. June paged me to come up front and retrieve it. Not expecting any packages, I carried the box back to my desk. An old, inky smell emanated from it as I separated the packing tape with the edge of my scissors. I opened it up and pulled the crumpled, yellowed newspapers out of the box and to my horror, it was another typewriter!

This machine was called an Underwood and had a beautiful red enamel finish with a wood grain pattern to part of it. I glanced around the office to see if anyone was looking and inserted a piece of paper into the machine. As soon as I did, it started typing! The message it left for me was:

JEFF, LEAVE THIS ON YOUR DESK. LET'S STAY IN TOUCH. –THOMAS

DENISE OSTLER

THE SURPRISE VISIT

ONCE UPON A TIME, IN THE KINGDOM OF KAIROS, THERE DWELT a kindly woman named Tula who did cleaning and repairs at the Royal Infirmary. Tula worked hard and was tired every night. Although she was spent, Tula slept fitfully because no matter how hard she worked, the matron in charge wanted more from her. Tula worried that she wasn't doing enough, that she would never be able to satisfy Matron.

Tula went to Lady Hope's Art Gallery every Saturday to get inspiration for doing her own paintings of legendary creatures called turtlebats. No one had ever really seen one, but Tula had a keen imagination.

Tula walked across the village every Sunday to look after her aging aunt, Nona. For some unknown reason, Tula dreaded these visits. She always felt elated as she walked home from Nona's cottage on Borderline Path, but the dread slowly crept up on her again during the week.

After months of practice, at last a painting was good enough to show to Lady Hope. Tula wrapped it in brown paper, tied it up with kitchen string, and took it to the gallery on Saturday afternoon. She waited shyly while Lady Hope unwrapped the painting.

"This is lovely," exclaimed Lady Hope. "I will give you twenty gold pieces for it. Really my dear, you must go to Kairos City where you could sell many more of these."

"Thank you so much, my lady," said Tula. "But I could never leave my ailing aunt on her own. I am the only family she has left."

"I understand," said Lady Hope. "But if you change your mind, I am going myself by carriage on Monday morning. I can introduce you to gallery owners and set you up with a good life there."

Tula took the gold pieces home and put them in the cookie jar with her savings. She marveled at the sum, for it was more than she earned each week at the infirmary.

It was Sunday, and Tula walked through the town square on her way to Nona's house on Borderline Path. She carried a heavy satchel full of food slung across her chest. She stopped to rest a few minutes at the new coffee vendor's stand called "Kafi's Coffees." Kafi was an easygoing man and everyone in the village liked him.

A man who looked like a younger version of Kafi greeted Tula and served her a cup. "Where is Kafi today?" she asked.

"Kafi is my father and he is trusting me to run the stand today," the young man proudly answered. "Safe journeys, my lady."

Tula walked out to Borderline Path and let herself into Nona's cottage. Nona was looking healthy today, but she wore her nightgown with a shawl across her shoulders and sat crumpled in a chair. Tula greeted Nona and laid out the food on the kitchen table.

"Oh, I couldn't possibly have solid food now. I've been sick all week, and I haven't eaten for days," she frowned. "I need you to make me some cocoa."

Tula warmed the milk and stirred in the cocoa powder with sugar. She brought the cup to Nona and tried to cheer her by sharing the news about selling a painting. "I finished a turtlebat painting and you'll never guess what happened . . ."

"No one has ever seen a turtlebat," interrupted Nona. "You are so simple. I need you to go to the market now and buy me some candles."

Tula was only too happy to go back out, and she took her time getting to the market where she purchased a packet of candles. On her return, she met Kafi on the road. He was carrying a big bouquet of flowers. He greeted her.

"What sweet flowers," said Tula. "Where are you going, sir?"

"I am paying a surprise visit to my new lady-friend. Her name is Nona."

Tula gulped and kept walking next to Kafi. "I've heard of this lady," she managed to say. "Isn't she quite frail?"

"Oh no," Kafi grinned. "She is very young at heart. We have dinner three times a week. On Saturday nights we drink ale and dance at the tavern. Last night was especially romantic. I just had to bring her flowers."

When they arrived at Borderline Path, Tula took the packet of candles out of her satchel and handed them to Kafi. "I have a feeling your lady-friend will like these," she said, trying to sound normal. "I'll be on my way now. I just remembered I left a pot on the stove at home."

Tula turned and walked briskly back into town. She stopped at the infirmary's front desk and resigned her post. When she got home, she went next door to tell the landlord she was moving. She packed some clothes into her satchel with her little box of paints and a few paintbrushes. Tula emptied her savings from the cookie jar into her purse and went to bed. She slept soundly and dreamed of turtlebats flying under a full moon.

The next morning, Tula met Lady Hope in front of the gallery and boarded the carriage with her, bound for Kairos City. As they slowly passed her old house, Tula spied Nona and Matron standing at the door. A "For Rent" sign was already placed in the window. Tula hid her face but she could still hear them talking.

"It took me all day to walk here," whined Nona. "She left without even saying farewell."

"The same here," said Matron crossly. "What an ungrateful woman. Don't worry, Nona, I will look after you on Sundays."

Tula and Lady Hope held their breath until they were out of earshot, and then burst out laughing. As she watched the scenery go by, Tula had the strangest feeling. "I know that I have done my best for others, and I have given enough," she said. "But I don't know what this new feeling is . . ." and her voice cracked.

"What is it my dear?" asked Lady Hope.

Tula smiled behind her tears. "I feel free."

JAN FISHER

TWO-THIRTY-NINE
1968

GRITTY, DISHEVELED, AND DOWNRIGHT DANGEROUS, THE Lower East Side of Manhattan became home once the Army discharged me in the late '60s. "Loisaida," the Latinos called it; tenements with rusted out fire escapes and sprawling projects streaked with graffiti were home to anyone who could pay low rents. Condemned buildings housed squatters and abandoned lots and parks the city didn't care about turned into shanty towns that sheltered the otherwise homeless. The beats and the artists added their own flair. The hippies came in with peace and love. Together with the hepcats, who gathered in little bars and dives and played music all night long, they created what I considered a haven below 14th Street. A guy like me fit right into this steaming pot of passion, desperation and flamboyance. Everything I needed was her.

Days, I went to City College on the Bill. Nights, I chased the music. As a sax player, I hit every jazz gig possible. And if they invited me to play my horn, I called that heaven. Me, an ex-GI with the worst behind him, I hoped, young, black and proud enough. Even though I lived dirt cheap, and there were moments when I barely hung on, that never bothered me. On this night, with a pocket full of change and one single, I wasn't flush but I knew how to squeeze a nickel until the buffalo crapped. I had made it somehow, sane, intact and militarily emancipated.

When they were drafting during Vietnam, I was under the age limit for exemption, unmarried, and not in school, so I didn't stand a snowball's chance in h-e-double hockey sticks, ya dig? My name came up and that was that. Leastwise, I didn't get Nam. I remember looking at that Army paper they gave me when I finished up basic training at Dix, only they don't call it a paper. They call it "orders," because once they got you, everything's an order. You got no freedom anymore. They called me "private," but I had no privacy either. Jumpy with nerves, could hardly focus, but I saw my name in print, "Calvin Edgar Jones." Then I saw the word, "Germany," and my knees nearly buckled in relief. I read it over a bunch a times 'cause I could hardly believe it.

From then on I was shuffled around and did what they told me to do. I'm not a big guy, but I'm broad shouldered and muscular and know how to keep my mouth shut, so I figured that even for a black kid I'd be awright. I heard all the stories comin' outta Nam and saw some of the guys I grew up with. Most that came back got screwed up something awful, bodies or minds or both, and heavy into drugs. I never got into the drugs. I didn't like needles or swallowing pills. I smoked marijuana once. Didn't do a damn thing for me and I didn't like the smell or taste. Mostly I didn't like losing control, I think. It wasn't easy living with the ones that did. Couple times I sold my urine, but it made me feel too guilty so I turned down all kinda money then and it didn't help my popularity none. I won't say I didn't drink some, but I had no need to go overboard, ya dig? And I stayed outta scenes where somebody'd want to slug me just because they were drunk and I was black. Plenty who were sober wanted to slug me and that was bad enough.

My grandmother, Amelia Augustine Jones, raised me in the little Hudson River town of Ossinging where the prison is, what they call Sing-Sing. I called my grandmother Ma, like my aunt and uncles did. My own mother, Ma's youngest, died when I was four. Ma taught me how to conduct myself, how to respect myself and told me about God. And did I ever have to watch my mouth. I only had the sting of Lifebuoy once to cure me and funny that it's pretty much stuck to this day. She wanted me to do right, and she said if I did, God would do right by me. I wanted to think so, but mostly, when I was growing up, I feared Ma's wrath more than God's. Don't get me wrong. She was a good woman and once she went home, as black folks refer to dying, I haven't had a day I didn't think about her. As a kid, I just had to mind her and never cuss or sass, but sometimes the boy in me came out and there was nuthin' I could do about it.

One time she sent me to the store. I played around on the way, climbing fences, jumping off hillsides, walking on low walls, and I lost the five-dollar bill she gave me. I figured I was on death watch then and, at twelve years old, the only solution for me was to leave town. There sure was no goin' back without the groceries. Then an idea came to me. My grandmother's credit was good at this little store. So I charged the stuff and took 'em home like everything was normal. "There weren't no change, Ma. It was a little over and he said not to worry about it." I think it was the first and only time I got away with lying and that was either Ma or God giving me a break. I raked leaves for a month to pay the bill, a dollar at a time. I am convinced the reason I am alive today is because I paid that bill. Heck, the Army had nothing on Ma.

Once Uncle Sam liberated me, I shared a crib with my old high school buddies, Morton and Tommy, in the Loisida neighborhood they called Alphabet City, between Avenues C and D on 13th Street. We were pretty tough, but even so, it was taking a chance to live down there—break-ins, muggings and lots of rough stuff going down all the time. The only thing I had of value was my horn and they'd take it in a minute to pawn it. Drugs were everywhere. I mean, man, you were tripping over dealers and junkies on the street. I could protect myself and shoot a real evil look if I had to. You had to keep watch, know where you were and who was around you. And keep your place locked up tight. We were lucky the previous tenants of our place had bars put on the windows.

That was our only luxury. Our decrepit little fifth floor walk-up, what they called a railroad flat since the rooms connected like on a train, came with tenement décor, layer upon layer of paint chipping off the walls, holes in the floor that went clean through, and the only bathtub in the kitchen, right out in the open, but none of it bothered me. I was in the city and I could walk everywhere, even to uptown gigs. They'd pay me and I'd take the subway home.

But Greenwich Village was always my favorite—jazz everywhere. The place was swinging and I wanted to be around it all, keeping up my chops, getting known and getting a few gigs here and there, sometimes even a studio gig. Those paid the most. It took 'em forever to send you your pay, but if you kept at it, you'd be awright, ya dig?

On this Saturday night I didn't have a gig and I really wanted to get out and hear some music. I knew some cats were playing at the Village Tavern on Bleecker. No cover and I could get a couple fifty-cent drafts there. I counted what I had in my pocket. Two dollars and thirty-nine cents, what I had to my name. Two-thirty-nine. It wouldn't stretch far, but it could buy me an evening, and if I was careful I'd come home with change. I had to hear some tunes, and I hoped they'd let me play. I lived for the music.

First I needed to feed my stomach. Rummaging around in our desolate pantry, I saw some rice and a can of beans left from the last time I bought groceries. That was about the end of the food. Didn't have even a hambone or a scrap of fatback to flavor it, but I found a shriveled up pepper and a piece of onion in the fridge and cooked up that mess of rice and beans in my old cast iron pot, seasoning it with some dried red pepper flakes like Ma used to do. Hey, it wasn't half bad and it was a meal. I was more focused on the music anyhow.

I grabbed my sax, praying I'd be able to sit in at the club when they started the jam after the regular sets, left the crib and locked those locks up real tight, all three of them. Didn't matter how many times I set out like this, I always felt like a kid going to the county fair or something.

Right by Tompkins Square Park, I saw the guy coming toward me. Maybe it was nuthin' but you always watched out, ya dig? Lots of people were out that night. But it was dark by the park fence where I was walking and this dude had his eye on me and I didn't like it.

"Wha'd it look like, bro?" he asked, as he approached, a kinda scraggly lookin' white guy, maybe mid-thirties.

"Cool, man," I said it low, hoping he wasn't gonna stick me up or nuthin'. I only had the two-thirty-nine in my pocket and it might make him mad. Shoot, it made me mad.

"Hey, man, hold up a second," he kinda blocked my way. "I'm lookin' for some stuff, man. Can you get me some stuff?" While he was saying this, the cat actually flashed a fifty at me.

Man, I'll tell you that fifty looked good. I knew I could take it and take him, too, if I had to. I won't lie. Something else crossed my mind. I could take him to a building a couple blocks away where I knew how to go in the front and get out the back way. I could take the dough, have him wait, and he'd never see me again. Look, I wasn't raised that way. But sometimes you're at the end. And the landlord don't play when the rent's due. But even though he was a ratty lookin' loser, I couldn't do it. Just wasn't me. In fact, in about another second, I got angry. Plenty angry. I let him have it.

"Wha'd ya think? Every black guy is a drug dealer? Is that whacha think? Just because I'm down here and I'm black, you think I got some stuff to sell you? Get outta my way, you lousy junkie."

He jumped aside because I know he was thinking I was about to slug him. I had my fist balled up, and I was angry enough to do it. Partly because he was a junkie and he had money and I didn't. But I just kept walking, pretty fast, too. Didn't turn around but I sensed he wasn't following me. It occurred to me when I cooled down some that maybe the guy was a narc, trying to set me up. I didn't know, but I bet he was. The more I thought about it, the more sure I was. And I think his eyes wasn't dead looking. What with the horn case I was carrying, he probably saw I was a musician, too, and lots of them were users. I remembered hearing that kind of thing was going on down there, those set-ups by the narcs. Somebody I knew got busted. In the joint doing time for next to nothing.

Anyway, after a few more blocks or so, when I got to the corner of A and 7th Street, I got caught by some traffic. I looked down and thought I was seeing things. Right at my feet, on the curb, was a fifty-dollar bill. Geez, oh man! I looked around and there was nobody. At first I thought the narc planted it there to trap me, but that was kinda crazy and I wasn't about to let it go to the next guy. I acted like I was tying my shoe and scooped it up in a casual way, crumpled it in my hand, and didn't look at it.

I kept on my way and nobody messed with me all the way to the club. Just before I went in, I stood in a dark doorway, got the bill out my pocket to smooth it out. Sure enough, a genuine U.S. Mint fifty-dollar bill, the real deal. I was feeling more than a little paranoid and wanted to break that bill fast but easy like. Even though it was the Village and the scene was pretty hip, sometimes blacks were suspect anyway. When I stepped out onto the sidewalk, I half expected to feel the narc's hand on my shoulder and hear some trumped up charge, but nothing happened. I eased into the place and checked out the scene. The cats I'd come to hear play were just setting up and the barstools were about half full. I took one at the end near the wall where I had a good vantage point of the entire room, my usual caution. I liked to see what was coming at me at all times.

"Hey, man," I greeted the bartender, pleased to see he was a guy named Vince that I knew from a few times before. "Got some of that good port tonight?" When I had dough I knew how to live.

He showed me the bottle and it was the stuff, all right. "Right on, man, and lemme buy a round for the bar, whatever anybody's drinking," I told him. Well, shoot, I could see they most all had drafts. Everybody cheered me and I was in like Flynn for the rest of the night. That one round plus a generous tip didn't hardly cost me nuthin'. I got my fifty busted nice and easy, just the way I wanted it, got myself a pack of smokes, too, and I was real comfortable sitting there. After a few sets, it was getting late and some of the famous cats wandered in. This spot was known to play after hours and that's when things would start smokin'. Some of 'em knew me pretty well and asked me to sit in. It was a great night, kickin' it with the coolest cats around. And to top it off, two of 'em booked me for gigs uptown. Man, it was crazy.

I walked myself back home around three in the a.m. The streets were quiet, even for Loisaida. I patted my pocket with the folded bills, over thirty-five bucks left, and thought about how I'd buy some groceries to share with Morton and Tommy. They'd like a nice big steak and I'd roast up some sweet potatoes and bake a big pan of cornbread from Ma's recipe. Just as I was thinking about getting' a quart of tangy buttermilk that I'd sop up with the cornbread, I saw the shadow out the corner of my eye. I'd been walking fast so when something tripped me and something else hit me on the back of my head, I flew across the sidewalk and went down hard on my chest. It knocked the wind clean outta me. Somebody jumped on my back. Then I knew it was two of 'em. Before I could breathe or move, I felt my pockets rifled and heard 'em run. I thought I was gonna black out, but I managed to push myself off the sidewalk and air rushed back into my lungs. By the time I struggled to my feet, gasping, they were long gone.

I felt the spot on my head and I was bleeding a little but I'd live. I saw the board they hit me with. Probably kids or them skinny junkies. Made me real mad they took my money, the rest of the fifty and even the two-thirty-nine I didn't spend. But in the next thought I was glad they didn't have a tire iron or a knife. Or that the nails in the board didn't connect. Then I realized my hand no longer gripped my horn case. I spun around to look all over, but it was gone. Panic rose in my chest same time as the rage. Those filthy bastards took my horn. I let out a string of words I didn't even know I knew and smacked the telephone pole a few times. Damn, I loved that horn. This would set me back plenty, even if I scored one at the pawn shop. But without the gigs I didn't know how I'd save up. And without the gigs, without the music, I didn't want to think about it.

Back at the crib, everything was just as I left it. After I blotted my head with some alcohol, I lit the stove with a big wooden match and turned it on low to warm up the leftover rice and beans. I felt weak and empty, still angry but my rage fast turning into hopelessness. While my food was heating, I started sorting through a stack of mail that had accumulated on the table for a few days, mostly bills and stuff I didn't want to deal with.

I picked up an envelope with my name on it from a place I didn't recognize and slit it open with a table knife. Inside was a check made out to me. It was for some studio work I'd done, maybe a couple, three months ago, and forgot about. But here's the part that got me and will always get me. This check was for two hundred and thirty-nine dollars. Two-thirty-nine, like the little bit I had in my pocket early on, but move the period and add two zeros. I swear this is true on the grave of my grandmother.

I sat there and looked at that check for a long time while the evening played back in my mind, especially that run-in with the narc. My entire life coulda taken a whole different turn that night. Was I protected in a kinda crazy way? Felt like it. Not so much because I didn't do the wrong thing. But more than that, I think I was somehow told not to do the wrong thing, and I listened, ya dig? See, maybe Ma's still around somewhere. Well, I did see her a couple different times after she went home, but I don't expect you to believe that. I kept thinking how I didn't fall for the narc's setup. I got the fifty and even though I lost most of it, I had a great evening and a couple new gigs coming up. I got mugged but survived, barely injured. I'd buy a horn. I had a big fat check. For two-thirty-nine.

That two-thirty-nine was a sign to me. Now I'm not no saint or angel. I don't even consider myself religious like some folk. But I was told something by that sign, ya dig? I bet everybody gets a sign, at least once. You gotta train your brain to think of it that way. If everybody thought back, they'd remember they got a sign, sometime.

ABOUT THE CONTEST JUDGE

from http://www.thehealingseed.com/

Laura Hope-Gill founded the first Certificate in Narrative Healthcare Program in North Carolina in 2013 at Lenoir-Rhyne University in Asheville after attending Narrative Medicine training at Columbia University College of Physicians and Surgeons. In 2014 she was invited to co-author the Narrative Playbook produced by Robert Wood Johnson Foundation and now made available online to all practitioners. In 2013 she worked with Dr. Bruce Kelly at the Charles George V.A. in Asheville to pilot one of six programs in the nation in which World War II veterans' stories are included in the patient "file" ahead of the vital statistics; this program is now being replicated nationwide. In 2014, she assisted in launching the Poetic Medicine program at the Charles George V.A. which now presents an annual poetry reading by Vietnam Veterans. She has presented keynotes and workshops at Wake Forest School of Medicine, Appalachian State University Expressive Arts Annual Retreat, The National Association for Poetry Therapy Annual Conference, the Johnson City V.A., Lenoir-Rhyne and AHEC's Future of Medicine Conference at Lenoir-Rhyne, Health Union, and forthcoming Grand Rounds at Eastern Carolina University School of Medicine. She is currently working with MAHEC and Western Carolina Medical Society to develop a Narrative Healthcare Symposium on Witness-Fatigue for October 2019.

She holds an MFA in Creative Writing and is a North Carolina Arts Fellow and Poet Laureate of the Blue Ridge Parkway. She is author of *The Soul Tree: Poems and Photographs of the Southern Appalachians* with photographs by John Fletcher, Jr.

ABOUT THE AUTHORS

Grey Wolfe LaJoie

The author of "Bits of Sugar," first-place contest winner, is an MFA candidate at the University of Alabama. He was born and raised in Asheville. His literary pieces "Idly" and "Poetics" appeared in A.B. Tech's 2015 *Rhapsody*, a publication of which he was also editor. His later work can be found in *Jersey Devil Press*, *Michael Martone's Door*, *TalkingBook*, and his chapbook *A Commando in Floral Remembers His Mother*. He is capable of doing a variety of silly voices, and he will never leave you.

Spencer E. Stevens

The author of "Enough to Show" first became a published author at the age of eleven. She has since been apprentice at a publishing company as well as authored and edited for local newspapers including *Critter and Cougar Chronicles*. Her fiction has appeared in the women's literary journal *Minerva Rising* ("Angels," Dec. 2012), and in a prior anthology of short stories published by Grateful Steps THE CRICKET AND OTHER STORIES ("Moon Boy," 2014, a second-place winner). As an Electro-Mechanical Engineer and artist, she now helps business owners with their image and advertising. You can find more of her work at D3Design.org.

J.S. Sollazzo

The author of "Golden Years" was born in North Carolina in 1966. He has had short stories published by *Short Stories Bimonthly, Mudrock, Midnight Times, Toasted Cheese* and other publications. His short story "Doorbell," published by *The Story Teller,* was nominated for the 2005 Pushcart Prize. He placed second in the 2012 Grateful Steps Short Story Contest ("Small Lives") and placed first the following year in *The Cricket and other stories* with his story, "The Cricket." He and his wife live in Weaverville, North Carolina.

Robin Russell Gaiser

Robin Russell Gaiser, MA, CMP, holds degrees in English literature and psychology and a certificate in therapeutic music. "I'll Fly Away" is her third story to win a spot in a Grateful Steps short story contest anthology. *Open for Lunch* (Pisgah Press: 2018), her second memoir, was released in November 2018. Her first memoir, *Musical Morphine: Transforming Pain One Note at a Time* (Pisgah Press: 2016) was named a finalist in the Best Book Awards in 2017 by American Book Fest. In March 2018 she delivered a TEDx Talk entitled "Good Vibrations: Less Drugs, More Music." She has also published several short stories, essays and poems. She is a regular presenter at book clubs, book stores and professional groups. As a vocalist and multi-instrumentalist she has performed and recorded professionally; as a Certified Music Practitioner she provides live bedside acoustic music to the ill and dying in hospitals, hospices, nursing homes rehabs and private homes. She and her husband live in the beautiful mountains of Asheville, North Carolina. For TEDx Talk, general information and scheduling procedures access www.robingaiser.com.

Evan Williams

The author of "No Light" lives on the family apple orchard in the Blue Ridge mountains of Hendersonville, North Carolina. He became interested in writing in sixth grade after winning second place in an agriculture conservation essay contest. He received his M.F.A. at Queens University at Charlotte.

Evan Williams is author of *Angst,* a 2011 Kindle collection of poems that deals with the difficulties and triumphs of being human. He won a Willie Parker Peace Award, 2015, presented by The North Carolina Society of Historians for *One Apple at a Time,* Grateful Steps Publishing, Asheville, NC, 2014, nonfiction. In 2016, he was a winner in the International first annual Hemingway Shorts, short story contest, for his submission, "Surface Tension," published in *Hemingway Shorts,* a collection of new and engaged writing from new and engaged writers in the best tradition of Ernest Hemingway, published by The Ernest Hemingway Foundation of Oak Park, Oak Park, Illinois, 2016. He was a finalist for the poem "Roots Run Deep 'Round Here" in an Atlanta Review International Poetry Contest. He was a finalist, his short story appearing in a prior anthology published by Grateful Steps *THE CRICKET AND OTHER STORIES* ("Seventy-Two," 2014.)

Evan and his wife, Fonda, have six children between the ages of 31 and 15. They also share their home with several furry, four-legged family members. For more information, follow Evan's frequent postings at www.evanwilliamsauthor.com.

Bernie Brown

The author of "The Best Shot" lives in Raleigh, NC where she writes, reads, sews and watches birds. Her stories have appeared in *Modern Creative Living, Belle Reve, Still Crazy,* the *Raleigh News and Observer*, and several other publications. She has been nominated for a Pushcart Prize, is a Writer in Residence at the Weymouth Center and a member of Women's Fiction Writers Association. Her first novel was just accepted for publication by Moonshine Cove Publishing. Get to know her better at bablossom.wixsite.com/bernie-brown-writer.

Heath Towson

Heath Towson has been playing percussion for over fifteen years. He graduated from Appalachian State University with a degree in Music Industry Studies and Percussion. He plays with the Central United Methodist Brass Choir and the Asheville Community Band. Heath worked as a drum circle facilitator and tour guide for the Rhythm! Discovery Center in Indianapolis, teaching children and adults of all ages about percussion and rhythm. His time at Rhythm! was the inspiration for his book, *Lionel's Drum*, published by Grateful Steps in 2015.

Denise Ostler

The author of "Surprise Visit" is an artist and writer. Her images appear in the 2019 *We'moon Datebook: Gaia Rhythms for Womyn. Fanning the Flame*. Denise writes "fairy tale medicine" stories to engage and soothe the nervous system. You can read more stories and see art-work at www.facebook.com/ fairytalemedicine.

Jan Fisher

"Two-thirty-nine" is one of several interwoven stories in a book Jan Fisher is writing, *Mrs. Vargo's Honeymoon*. She began her writing career with Patuxent Publishing, a group of Maryland community newspapers. She later moved to New York City and continued to freelance for the Whitney Corporation's publications and others. She recently completed online theological studies at Princeton Seminary and is an associate pastor at the Jesus People Art and Worship Center in Asheville, North Carolina. She lives with her potter husband in Weaverville.

ABOUT THE CONTEST COORDINATOR

from http://douglasgibsonwrites.com/about/

Douglas Gibson was born in Greensboro, North Carolina, and attended Davidson College and the University of North Carolina. He and his wife, Stacey, and son, Griffin, live in lovely Asheville, North Carolina, along with a small dog named Spencer and a medium chicken named Juliet. When he isn't writing about books or designing them for other people, Douglas is usually hard at work writing books of his own. He is author of *Tales of a Fifth-Grade Knight,* published by Capstone Young Readers.

www.ingramcontent.com/pod-product-compliance
Lightning Source LLC
Chambersburg PA
CBHW071414170626
46811CB00003B/1397